DEATH ON THE DOURO

When wine writer Ezra Brant visits his friend Matthew Sykes' port farm — quinta — in Portugal's Douro Valley, it's an opportunity to research his book . . . However, after a series of suspicious accidents, he agrees to help his friend discover the truth behind them . . . But as he learns more about the book's subject, the port-shipper Joseph James Forrester, who drowned in 1861, Ezra believes that he was murdered. And when a murderer strikes in Sykes' quinta, the twin investigations into past and present intrigues come together in a shocking climax.

TONY ASPLER

DEATH ON THE DOURO

Complete and Unabridged

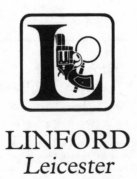

LINFORD
Leicester

First published in Great Britain

First Linford Edition
published 2006

The moral right of the author
has been asserted

All characters in this publication are fictitious
and any resemblance to real persons, living or
dead, is purely coincidental.

British Library CIP Data

Aspler, Tony, *1939 –*
Death on the Douro.—Large print ed.—
Linford mystery library
1. Brant, Ezra (Fictitious character)—
Fiction 2. Duero River Region (Spain
and Portugal)—Fiction 3. Detective and
mystery stories 4. Large type books
I. Title
813.5'4 [F]

ISBN 1–84617–186–5

Published by
F. A. Thorpe (Publishing)
Anstey, Leicestershire

Set by Words & Graphics Ltd.
Anstey, Leicestershire
Printed and bound in Great Britain by
T. J. International Ltd., Padstow, Cornwall

This book is printed on acid-free paper

To Ted Turner
who introduced me
to the Baron

Ezra could hear the screams of the drowning passengers above the rush and rage of the river.

The chocolate-coloured water churned and lashed at the rocks as it raced towards the rapids. The upturned boat, its mast snapped and its square canvas sail spreading like a tablecloth across the surface of the angry water, was already sinking into the grade of the cataract.

From his vantage point high above the canyon Ezra could see the tragedy unfold below him. Men and women desperately flailing for the rocky shore, their hands cut and bleeding from trying to grasp the sharp granite boulders as the current swept them towards the rapids.

One man clung to a floating barrel that suddenly disintegrated as it hit a rock, releasing a deluge of olive oil under which he disappeared without a sound.

The boatman, a great ox of a man in

black breeches and a shirt the colour of blood, had made the shore and stood dripping on the rocks, his massive chest heaving as he gasped for air. He held a long pole in his hands. He stretched it out towards another man who was thrashing in the water below him. Ezra could see the determination in the drowning man's face as he tried to grab the end of the pole. His thin lips were pursed; his black hair was plastered to his forehead like a helmet. Droplets of water glistened in his chinstrap beard.

Ezra knew that face; he had seen it before and he could not remember where. A photograph perhaps.

The river seemed to suck at the heels of the drowning man but he fought against its force.

Ezra tried to shout his encouragement but no sound came. Only the howl of the wind and the water's roar.

The man's fingers almost touched the pole but he was driven away from the shore by the power of the torrent. The boatman inched to the edge of the rocks and held the pole at arm's length and called, 'Baron, Baron!'

The man was going down but he kicked his legs frantically to buoy himself up, his head breaking above the frenzy of the waves. His will to survive had given him strength. He reached up and grasped the end of the pole with one hand.

The boatman began to drag him into shore yet still he only held the pole with his left hand; the right, unseen below the water, appeared to be holding his waist as if he was pressing a wound. He kept shouting to the boatman who was hauling him in like a great fish.

A few feet from shore the boatman stopped pulling and changed the position of his feet on the rocks. He looked around him and then raised the angle of the pole. His face contorted and he began to push downwards. The end of the pole was lodged in the man's waistcoat. He began to submerge, releasing his grip around the pole. A stream of bubbles broke to the surface where he had gone under. The boatman kept the pressure on the body to keep it below the surface.

Ezra shouted and tried to make his way

down the rocky slope but there was no path to the water's edge. The boatman held the man under, the muscles in his shoulders bulging with the effort. The pole jerked a few times and then it was still. The boatman scanned the shore for survivors and then looked up at Ezra, shielding his eyes from the sun.

He was laughing.

'Look, Ezra Brant,' he called, his voice echoing above the water's roar. 'Mark it well. This is the place where the Baron de Forrester drowned. The Devil's Cauldron . . . '

★ ★ ★

A sudden lurch followed by the piercing sound of a whistle awakened Ezra.

The train had stopped at Régua, the town on the western edge of port wine country. He looked out of the dusty window to the barrack-like row of wine-company warehouses along the river that swelled at this point where the River Corgo flowed into the Douro.

The heat of a September afternoon and

4

the effects of lunch at the Factory House in Oporto had left him drowsy. The motion of the train, the stuffiness of the carriage and the soporific effect of the port had taken their toll. Ezra had nodded off and the thoughts that had preoccupied him in his waking hours now played themselves back in dream form.

The Devil's Cauldron. That's what his host, the courtly Matthew Sykes, had called the rapids where the Baron de Forrester — the most famous or infamous Englishman in the history of port, depending on whom you listened to — had met his death in 1861.

They were standing by the fireplace in the Factory House map room after lunch, looking up at the ten-foot-long topological plan of the River Douro. It had been created by Forrester who had spent twelve years surveying, charting and documenting one hundred and forty miles of the river from Vilvestre in Spain to the point where its waters empty into the Atlantic at Foz do Douro.

Forrester's map marked every indentation of the river's shoreline, cited two hundred and ten rapids, listed the ferries and pinpointed seventy-nine quintas (wine farms). His incredible feat of cartography earned him his Barony from King Ferdinand II. In England he was known as the Baron de Forrester.

'That's our quinta there, Quinta do Santo Pedro. Been in the family for two hundred years,' said Matthew Sykes, indicating its position on the map with the diffidence of an Englishman who is proud — but not vainglorious — of his family's long history in the region.

He was wearing his customary three-piece suit, in spite of the heat outside, a regimental tie and a gold watch chain looped between the pockets of his waistcoat. He was pointing to a bend in the river above the town of Pinhão.

'Of course, the river's different now. They've blasted the rocks to make navigation easier and they've put in a series of dams to get rid of the rapids. Here, at Cachao de Valeira where Forrester was drowned, it's like a millpond now. There's a hydro-electric dam there.'

★ ★ ★

Ezra had been commissioned to write a book about port and was touring Portugal to do the final research. He had contacted his friend, Matthew Sykes, who had written a monograph on his own company and was respected by the English shippers as the most knowledgeable professional in the trade regarding the history of the British in Oporto.

A year previously Ezra had flown to London for a tasting of Canadian wines and had phoned Sykes in Oporto to ask for his assistance. His secretary had told him that Sykes was currently in London for meetings and could be contacted at the Connaught Hotel. When Ezra phoned him there the shipper had invited him to the Garrick Club for a drink. From the depths of worn leather armchairs the two men had discussed port for the whole afternoon while sipping on Macallan eighteen-year-old malt whisky.

'Ask a Portuguese what is port and he will tell you one thing. Ask an Englishman and he'll tell you another,' Ezra remembered him saying. 'To the Portuguese, port is tawny, a wine fortified with brandy and left to age in wood for ten, twenty, forty years. That's the way they like it. The Englishman's wine is vintage port, bottled after two years and left to mature in the bottle. Of course, that's only in declared years, as you know. It's a whole different drink. Different flavour, different mouth feel, my boy.'

It amused Ezra that Sykes kept referring to him as 'my boy', since he could not have been more than ten years his senior — a man in his early sixties, spare of frame, gaunt of face who seemed to fold himself into three as he lowered himself into the armchair. Compared to Ezra's bulk, unruly white hair and rubicund face, Sykes had the ascetic look of a scholar-monk rather than a purveyor of beverage alcohol. He reminded Ezra of an English master he had had at Trinity who tried to teach him cricket, convinced that the left-handed Ezra could be a bowler of googlies, whatever that meant.

'Next year, we're celebrating our 200th anniversary,' said Sykes, during a lull in the conversation. 'My great-great-grandfather, after whom I was named, bought the quinta in 1797, two years after the end of the French Revolution. A Sykes has run it ever since. Perhaps you'll come and help us celebrate?'

The invitation was tossed off in such a casual manner, rather as if he had said, 'You must come to dinner soon,' that Ezra merely nodded his thanks and thought no more about it. Three months later a square envelope plopped through the letterbox of his house in North Toronto. Inside was a gilded card formally inviting him to attend the four-day anniversary celebration at the Quinta do Santo Pedro. The dates coincided with the grape harvest.

Inside the envelope was a handwritten note in an energetic hand:

My dear Ezra, I do hope you can attend our little bash. I have taken the liberty of having our travel agent in London contact you to arrange your flight details from Toronto to Oporto via Lisbon. I suggest that you overnight in Oporto before taking the train up to the Douro. If you agree we will book your hotel and have your train ticket awaiting you at the desk.

As a lover of port, and one who has a professional interest in the health of the trade, I'm sure you will learn much from participating in the vintage (and let's hope that the trade can declare this one. Heaven knows we've gone too many years without one) and such a trip can only make your writings more authentic.

In order to entice you to accept our invitation I should tell you that our vineyard manager found a bundle of old letters in a dovecot on the property last week which pur-port, at first glance, to be the correspondence of Joseph James Forrester. My travels have prevented me from studying the documents but perhaps they may be of use to you for your book. I will gladly put them at your disposal in return for a modest mention on the acknowledgement page and an autographed copy of your work when it is published.

I look forward to hearing from you.

Yours sincerely,
Matthew Sykes

p.s. It goes without saying that this invitation is extended to your lady as well.

Ezra reread the letter trying to determine whether he was supposed to buy the air ticket or whether his host was offering to fly him to Portugal all expenses paid. The wording could be read either way. Wine writing was not a lucrative job. The lifestyle was enormously attractive, travelling the world in pursuit of the grape, being wined and dined in ancient châteaux, entertained by winemakers at the best restaurants, attending conferences and judging competitions in exotic places; but the financial rewards were slim. His weekly column in the *Toronto Examiner* paid a derisory amount but at least it gave him the profile to do other things. Consulting, preparing wine lists, training waiting staff in wine service. But could he afford to spend four days in Portugal at his own expense? Ever cautious with money, Ezra reflected on his situation.

The wine writer's lifestyle was seductive but he and his colleagues were not — and could never be — part of the wealth and grandeur that they experienced vicariously for short periods of time in the great estates of Europe or the shiny new wineries of California. And sometimes he felt that he existed on the periphery of the wine trade, feeding off it like a flea on a show dog. Rather like those birds that ride on the backs of rhinos, whose presence is tolerated because they eat the ticks that bother their hosts. Winery owners need wine writers to praise their products; publicity sells. Even criticism is better than having your wine ignored by the press.

In his brighter moments Ezra did not see himself as a wine *critic* but rather an evangelist for wine. He wanted his readers to share his passion, believing that wine in moderation was the healthiest of beverages. Take water, for instance, he had written in a recent column. Filthy stuff. No one has ever contracted cholera or yellow fever from drinking wine. Or milk: if it's not full of Strontium 90, it's riddled with organisms, a bacteria cocktail masquerading as white innocence. Wine, on the other hand, is Nature's own balm and were it not for the residual pall of Prohibition that has left governments and healthcare professionals with the psychological spectre of the Demon Drink wine would be prescribed as medicine for whatever ails you. St Paul got it right in his first epistle to Timothy: 'Drink no longer water, but use a little wine for thy stomach's sake and thine often infirmities.'

Ezra's often infirmity was a swelling of the ankles from spending too much time on his feet in tasting rooms. Otherwise he had the constitution (and the stomach) of a horse. Once he had eaten cow's udders in a restaurant in Gattinara, followed by donkey stew. Both were local delicacies. He had swallowed deep-fried insects in

Hong Kong, chewed on slabs of rendered pork fat as white and thick as sliced bread in a Hungarian cellar and sipped palm wine with a tribal chief on the Ivory Coast. Nothing upset him. Except Bird's Eye custard.

He checked his diary. There was the possibility of a trip to Greece to see the new vineyards around Thessaloniki but that could be postponed. The manuscript for his book on port was meant to be delivered to the publisher by the end of the year and he had barely started it. The trip to the Douro would give him the impetus he needed to complete it. And he would have access to Baron de Forrester's letters. Perhaps, through them, he could gain new insights into the development of the Englishman's drink and shed more light on the shipper's death.

Matthew Sykes had extended an invitation to his 'lady'. Ever delicate, the Englishman had used a phrase that could encompass a wide range of relationship options, as long as the partner who accompanied him was female. Ezra had not shared details of his private life with the older man. When they were not talking port together they spoke of mutual friends. Of rugby, how England fared in the Triple Crown, the Boat Race (which Ezra watched on television every year) and horse racing. As if by an unspoken contract between them the closest they came to personal revelations was while discussing their mutual preference for claret over red Burgundy ('More reliable, old boy. Claret's a wife, steady and predictable. Burgundy's a mistress. Volatile, cunning, exciting. Wonderful one day, an absolute disaster the next').

Ezra had neither wife nor mistress. His divorce from Connie had become absolute and though he was free to choose a companion he rather enjoyed his solitude. There was nothing to distract him from his work, no jolts from an emotional cattle-prod, no worrying over forgotten anniversaries of spurious moments (the day we met, the first restaurant we ate in, the first time we made love), no fussing over clothes . . . Still, he did miss the glow of a woman's skin by candlelight, the pressure of a hand in his, the brush of hair against his cheek when dancing and that moment when he knew they would end up in bed together for the first time. Now that was something to celebrate.

But there was no-one in his life at the moment. The wives of friends had tried to fix him up in the beginning. He accepted their invitations to dinner knowing that the fourth chair would be occupied by a single woman selected for him by his hostess.

Invariably, he would return home to the house in North Toronto alone, having dropped off the woman in question, refusing her verbal or physical blandishments to come up for a coffee. He usually said that he had to take the baby-sitter home but Michael was seventeen now and heaven knows where he spent his evenings. But there was Steppenwolf the beagle and Enoch the cat to be fed.

Ezra went straight to the computer and composed a reply to Sykes. He waited until after 6 p.m. to fax the message to Portugal as it was cheaper then.

Six weeks before the day of his flight to Oporto he received a fax from Matthew

Sykes: 'It occurs to me that you may require more time to study the Forrester letters which are most intriguing. You may also want a quiet place away from telephones and fax machines to write your book. I would like to suggest that you come a week earlier than arranged — before my other guests arrive and the festivities for our 200th-anniversary celebration get underway. I would esteem it a great honour to have you under my roof if you would agree to come and stay, accompanied or alone as you wish. I must confess I have my own selfish reasons for pressing this invitation upon you. I do hope that your schedule will permit the extra time away from Toronto. Please contact me as soon as possible.'

Intrigued by the seeming urgency of the message, Ezra phoned Sykes immediately and said he would be delighted to come. Over the transatlantic line he could hear the older man breathe a deep sigh of relief.

'I shall meet you in Oporto. We will lunch together at the Factory House.'

'Terrific, I've always wanted to see the

place. But tell me,' said Ezra, 'what is the selfish reason you want me there?'

There was silence for a moment as if the older man on the other end of the line was looking around the room before replying.

Then he said: 'Company.'

★ ★ ★

The Factory House, built in 1790 on what is now the Rua Nova dos Inglezes in Oporto, is the nearest thing you can get to a London club abroad. Its stark granite façade in Georgian style is as discreet and unostentatious as the doings of the British Association which occupies it. The British Association is an organization of twelve leading port shippers and their Factory has been the hub of British social life in Oporto for more than 160 years. Members gather for balls in the chandeliered ballroom with its musicians' gallery and they dine under a portrait of the reigning monarch at a mahogany table (accommodating forty-six) in the dining room. At the end of formal dinners members and their guests retire to the dessert room with an equally vast mahogany table and assume the same places as at dinner to pass the vintage port.

Ezra had read much about the Factory House and was as thrilled to enter its portals as he might have been, years earlier, to gain access to the dressing room of the Toronto Maple Leafs.

As treasurer of the British Association, Matthew Sykes was obliged, for the year of his office, to supply the Factory House with its tawny and white port requirements (each member once elected had to present fourteen cases of their firm's vintage port, equivalent to a quarter of a cask, for the Factory House cellar); and it fell to the treasurer to choose the vintage port for the Wednesday lunch. The members help themselves from unmarked decanters placed on the sideboard and speculate on the vintage and the shipper. Ezra had guessed that the port in his glass was a '77 and he knew that Sykes was too polite to serve him his own company's port, lest he be considered by his peers to be overly commercial, so he hazarded who the unknown shipper might be.

'I think it may be the best port of the vintage. If you don't mind me saying. I think it's Warre.'

'Absolutely right, old boy!'

Matthew Sykes slapped him on the back.

'You should be in the trade.'

'You mean switch from poacher to gamekeeper?' laughed Ezra, a little befuddled from the effects of two large glasses on top of his jet lag.

'It's after two,' said Sykes. 'The members can smoke now so if you've had enough port why don't we step outside.'

Since there were a couple of hours before his train left for the Douro, Matthew Sykes proposed that they go for a walk along the river. He had not broached the subject he had hinted at in his note to Ezra, nor had he displayed any unease that would have led Ezra to suspect the nature of the conversation he was about to have.

The sun was hot on Ezra's back. He wished he had remembered to take a hat.

He would need one in the Douro. He waited for Sykes to initiate the conversation as they made their way down the cobbled street to the Praça da Ribeira, a square that opened onto the quay, where tourists lunched under large white umbrellas. Across the river that reflected the blueness of the sky was Vila Nova de Gaia. Ezra could see the long, white, barrack-like port lodges with their red-tiled roofs rising in graduated steps up the slope of the hill. Each was emblazoned with the name of the company. Moored off the quay was a series of *barcos rabelos*, like large flat-bottomed gondolas with pipes of port stacked on their decks, their square sails furled and their long rudders angling up to a high poop deck. Ezra committed their shape and construction to memory: it was in such a riverboat that the Baron de Forrester had met his fate.

They were walking along the quay past upturned rowboats and fishing nets that smelled of brine and herring. Laundry, blindingly white in the sun, hung lifeless from lines strung along the weathered stone retaining wall. Ahead of them, spanning the river, was a railway bridge supported by a rainbow-shaped arc of iron. There was something about its shape that reminded Ezra of some other architectural line he had seen elsewhere.

'That's the Dom Luis I bridge,' said Sykes, shielding his eyes from the sun with a hand. 'The Portuguese are very proud of it. It was designed by Eiffel.'

Ezra studied the graceful iron parabola on which the bridge seemed to sit with the lightness of a kiss. His attention was suddenly diverted by a flash of light from the base of the bridge about 200 metres away — as if someone had flashed a mirror in his eyes. He looked in that direction and saw a man removing a telescopic lens from his camera. He wore baggy fatigue pants, army boots and a sleeveless jacket with myriads of pockets — the kind favoured by photographers on assignment.

'Do you know that man?' Ezra asked, turning to his companion.

'What man?'

When he looked again there was no

one. The man had vanished.

'What did you see?'

'Someone was taking a photo of us, I'm sure of it. The sun glinted off the lens when he moved it.'

'Probably just a tourist,' replied Sykes, and he half-turned so that he was facing the opposite bank. 'If you look up there, about three tiers, you can see our lodge. You can't see the name from here, unfortunately, just the roof.'

As Ezra squinted across the river, looking for the lodge, he wondered when Sykes would get around to bringing up the subject that was obviously uppermost in his mind. He decided to force the issue.

'I got the impression from your letter that there was something bothering you, Matthew. If I'm prying tell me, but if I can help . . .'

Sykes mopped a furrowed brow with a silk handkerchief he pulled from the breast pocket of his linen jacket. He coughed as a priest might before a sermon.

'Let's sit down in the shade somewhere

and have a cup of coffee.'

They climbed the steps to the Cais dos Guindais and found an outdoor café. Sykes ordered two coffees. The waiter, seriously moustached, hesitated and then nodded. Even to Ezra's untutored ear Sykes spoke execrable Portuguese. The little of the language he knew he had picked up in Toronto's Kensington Market and the rustic restaurants along Augusta Street where the expatriates gathered to eat cod with red wine, sing Fado and complain about Canadian winters.

When the coffees arrived Sykes looked around at the other tables and then leaned forward.

'I would like to take you into my confidence. What I am about to tell you is for your ears only. I am trusting you as a friend because there are situations occurring here that I cannot even raise within my own family. Do I have your word that you will put aside your journalist's hat for the moment?'

'Of course.'

'You may have realized that I have

24

made no mention of my wife, Amanda. The reason is that she will not be at the quinta to greet you. We are, in fact, separated after twenty-eight years of marriage. I won't go into the reasons. Suffice it to say she hates the Douro and has sworn never to set foot in Santo Pedro again. In any event, it seems she prefers the air-conditioned comfort of our flat in Lisbon and her bridge-playing friends there to her true place by my side. My son Luke has taken it very badly and he blames me. Naturally. Luke runs the day-to-day operations at the quinta.'

'Is he the winemaker?'

'Yes. He has an excellent palate and he and I make the final barrel selection for blending. We've been arguing a lot lately about the direction we should be going as a firm. Luke wants an annual release but we've always followed the trade and declared a vintage only in good years.'

'So he wants to put out a vintage bottling every year like Taylor's Quinta de Vargellas.'

'Yes, but Taylor's has the luxury of doing both. Declaring a vintage under their label and offering a single quinta wine every year under the farm name. All we have is our own quinta.'

'And you want me to talk to Luke?'

Sykes sighed.

'That is not why I invited you here although I would be obliged if you would.'

Sykes paused and placed a hand on Ezra's sleeve.

'The wine world may be global but it is very small. As owners of properties we all know each other. We all have importing agents in various countries and naturally we like to feel we're in good company on their lists. Prestige by association, as it were. We exchange our wine for Bordeaux or Burgundy, Champagne, good Hock and even — and this will surprise you — some Californian and Australian wines. I have Robert Mondavi Pinot Noir Reserve in my cellar and some Grange. I can't get over what those fellows charge for their wines. Frightfully expensive, but very good, I'm told. The point is one hears things and I've heard about you. Not your wine writing, although I know you're well respected, but your — how shall I call it?' — your sleuthing abilities. And your discretion.'

Ezra tried to stifle a smile. He had not considered himself a sleuth although he had found himself involved in a couple of murders that he had managed to solve before the local police — one in Beaujolais, the other in the Piedmontese hill town of Barbaresco. It seemed he was getting himself a reputation.

'As you know,' Sykes continued, 'our firm is celebrating its 200th anniversary. We have invited many guests from abroad as well as colleagues here in the Douro and civic dignitaries. We have been planning this party, if you will, for over a year. But as soon as I announced that I was going to have this event things started happening around the farm.'

'What sort of things?'

'Strange, rather bizarre episodes. The day after my announcement the doves in the dovecot suddenly died *en masse*. Vasco, my vineyard manager, found them lying on the roof, rotting in the sun. He thinks they were poisoned. It was when

27

he went inside to investigate that he found a bundle of Forrester's letters. They were wrapped in an old oilskin and wedged between the beams.'

'Was that the only death?'

'No. The housekeeper's dog, a stray mongrel she had been feeding, was found behind the fermentation vat with its throat cut.'

'Was there any message left? Any warnings?'

'No.'

'What else?'

'Nothing you can put your finger on. Pumps that broke down for no reason, fuses missing from the fuse box in the cellar. A cross painted in blood on the back wall of the chapel.'

'Do you have any disgruntled employees?'

'Not to my knowledge. We've always treated them very well. Most of them have been with us a long time. They're all very loyal, good workers. They invite us to their weddings and confirmations. The cook's eldest daughter, Rosa, just named her first son after me.'

'What about casual labour? The people who pick for you. Have you fired anyone?'

'They queue up to work for us, Ezra. We pay more than the other quintas because we only want the best grapes. They come back year after year for Gertrudes' food.'

'Have you called in the police?'

'I don't want the local police. I can only tell them what I have told you. It's a very tight community and I don't want there to be gossip. Although by now I imagine it's up and down the valley. Besides, the local police are hardly Scotland Yard.'

Sykes paid for the coffees and they began to walk up into the city towards the railway station where Ezra had already checked his suitcase.

They arrived, perspiring from the climb, at the base of the Cathedral. Its twin towers, like giant grey pepper pots, rose majestically into a cloudless sky. The massive rose window, set high above the west door, under Moorish castellation as curved as dragon's teeth, glowed like a vast opal in the sun.

Matthew Sykes talked about the sights around them, their history and their meaning to him personally. Having volunteered the information about the quinta he now seemed reluctant to pursue the subject. Ezra was determined to draw him out further.

'So you think someone is trying to sabotage your celebration?' he said, during a pause in the shipper's monologue.

'Too many things have gone wrong to be mere coincidence. And each episode seems to escalate from the last. The dog was bad enough but now I'm afraid someone might get hurt.'

'What exactly do you want me to do?' Ezra asked.

'I've let it be known that you are coming to stay at Santo Pedro to do research for your book. It will only be natural for you to be inquisitive. You can ask questions without arousing suspicion. They'll expect you to poke around the place. So if you keep your eyes open you might find out who's behind all this unpleasant business.'

He paused and looked up at the imposing façade of the Cathedral.

'They have terrible trouble with the pigeons, you know. Something in their excrement is eating away the stones . . . You don't have to do this, of course. I'm aware that the situation is potentially dangerous but I don't want to have to cancel our little party at the eleventh hour. I just want matters to go on as if nothing is wrong. Would you do this for me?'

Sykes placed his hands on Ezra's shoulders and looked him directly in the eye as if to elicit his co-operation before he spoke.

From what the Englishman had told him it did seem as if the string of incidents had been planned to create the maximum disturbance.

'Do you have a list of the people who work for you?'

Sykes smiled and reached into his jacket pocket.

'I thought you might ask for that so I had one drawn up. It gives all their names, how long they've worked for me

31

and what their duties are.'

'What about your guest list?'

'My guest list?'

'The people you've invited for the event.'

Sykes looked puzzled for a moment and then he nodded grimly.

'That's a terrible thought. I've been in the trade for over forty years, Ezra, dear boy, and I'm still willing to give people the benefit of the doubt. These are my friends and colleagues, after all.'

'But you'll let me have the list.'

'I'll have my secretary fax it up to the quinta. It'll be there when you arrive.'

'And when are you coming?'

'I had hoped to accompany you on the train but I'm afraid I have some tedious meetings with bankers. That's the downside of my life but I'll look forward to seeing you tomorrow. Have a good trip.'

A telephone beeped and Matthew Sykes looked almost as startled as Ezra.

'Oh, that's my cellular phone. Luke bought it for me. Insists I carry it when I'm away from the property. Damn nuisance if you ask me. Excuse me for a moment . . . Hello?'

Sykes' affable expression became serious as he listened to the voice on the other end of the line. He said nothing until the caller had finished speaking.

'Yes. I will deal with it. Thank you.'

He closed the phone and slipped it back into its leather holster which was covered by his waistcoat.

'Lawyers. A little matter of business I have to deal with. Now we must get you on your train.'

★　★　★

The S. Bento railway station in the centre of Oporto is built like a palace. Its exterior grandeur is enhanced within by huge tiled murals in blue and white depicting dramatic scenes from Portugal's history.

Ezra, suitcase in hand, stood gazing up at them in wonder as the enormous hall resonated with the sound of heels clicking on the marble floor and the echoing monotone of the train announcer.

33

Ezra loved train stations. The excitement of the anticipated journey is not compromised by the stomach-churning anxiety he always experienced at airports. There is a certain luxury, he felt, about travelling slowly and having the opportunity to observe the countryside. The rhythm of a train's movement and the sound of steel on steel induced relaxation and contemplation.

But the effects of lunch and the walk in the sun made his eyes feel heavy. He had intended to use the time to work on his book but the swaying movement of the first class carriage directly behind the engine, the hum of the wheels and the buzzing of the flies at the window soon lulled him to sleep. And he dreamed the nightmare of the Baron de Forrester's drowning.

At Régua he woke with a start, wondering if he had slept past his stop. In a panic he looked for the name of the station. Sykes had arranged for him to be met in Pinhão by his vineyard manager, Vasco, or the housekeeper Maria who would drive Ezra the twenty-kilometre journey up into the hills to the quinta.

Régua. Halfway there. Relieved, he settled back into his seat, trying to recall the dream he had had. It was so vivid, so real. He had immersed himself in the literature of port and the personalities that shaped the history of the trade. None was more attractive than the obstinate, uncompromising Yorkshireman, Baron de Forrester, whose controversial writings and brilliant draughtsmanship changed the nature and direction of the port trade. 'The saviour of the Douro' the press had called him in reporting his death. There were those, however, who saw Forrester as the Devil of Oporto.

Ezra took his suitcase down from the rack and opened it. He removed his laptop computer and turned it on. He called up a file named 'Baron' and read the few lines on the screen.

On May 12th, 1861, fifteen days shy of his fifty-second birthday, Joseph James Forrester, Baron of Portugal, or 'Joe' as he liked to be called, perished in the River Douro. Such was the love and respect accorded to him by his adopted country that the King of Portugal ordered the flags on the ships in the harbours of Lisbon and Oporto and those on the public buildings to be flown at half-mast. The river that he loved so dearly, that he had sketched and photographed and surveyed, had finally claimed him.

Ezra had written those words almost six months ago in his Toronto study with the snow thick on the windowsill and panes opaque with frost. Here, three thousand miles away from Toronto, in the heat and colour of the Douro, his prose seemed flat and lifeless to him.

In his dream he had seen Forrester struggle in the roaring torrents of the river which now stood like a millpond below him. He had seen Forrester's face, a face he now realized he had remembered from photographs at the Royal Photographic Society in Bath. To further his research Ezra had travelled there to see Forrester's photos of the river, the peasants of the Alto Douro and one poignant shot of the very bend in the river where he would meet his fate.

There was one photo in particular that had fascinated Ezra. It was a self-portrait of Forrester dressed in a frockcoat with velvet collar and lapels. He is standing in front of a curtain beside a large box of a camera, a small lens hanging from a ribbon around his neck like a monocle. His head is inclined towards the camera on top of which lies a black cloth. The powerful fingers of his left hand rest delicately on the camera's lens cap as if he is about to remove it; his right hand, out of sight, is placed behind the camera, the way a man might hold a woman with whom he is dancing. He looks directly into the lens that has captured him, his hooded eyes dreamy in sharp contrast to the hard, ironic line of his lips.

With his fleshy nose and corpulent features, his mop of shining, curly hair, his cleft chin almost hidden by a narrow band of beard, he has the sleek look of a successful mill owner rather than that of the man who revolutionized the port trade.

This was the man Ezra had seen in his dream being pushed under the waves by a boatman. Nowhere in his readings was there any suggestion that Forrester had been murdered. The received story was that the port shipper had been lunching at Quinta Vesúvio near the village of Numao, a majestic property belonging to his friend Dona Antonia Ferreira, a landowner of great prominence in the Douro.

Forrester's own boat was out of commission so the party of sixteen had taken a smaller craft. Among the other passengers were Baroness Fladgate, Dona Antonia and her husband, Francisco José da Silva Torres, and the Count and Countess of Azambuja (Dona Antonia's daughter and her husband). The small boat was hopelessly overloaded and Forrester told Torres he thought the rudder had been lashed the wrong way to negotiate the rapids at Valeira safely.

That Sunday in May, 1861, the river was running high and fast from torrential rains that had fallen unceasingly for two days prior to the accident, swelling its volume. As the boat moved swiftly into the narrows, the speed of the river increased, carrying it towards the rocks on the shore. The boatman's correction turned the prow towards the cataract but the hull struck a rock which caused it to overturn, snapping the mast.

All the women were rescued. The air trapped in their crinolines kept them afloat until they were washed ashore on a small beach downriver from the gorge.

Joseph Forrester had been wearing high boots which filled with water and weighed him down. He was a strong swimmer but he was weakened by a glancing blow from the falling mast. Barely conscious, he began swimming. Observers say he reached the shore and held onto a rock but the force of the current tore him loose.

His body was never recovered but there were rumours in the valley that a peasant had pulled in the floating corpse upriver near Pinhão, robbed it of a gold watch and money belt and rolled it back into the river.

That was the story.

There were also rumours among his enemies in Oporto that Forrester was a spy for the British Government. Others had hinted darkly that he was in the pay of the French. His solo treks deep into the Douro valley — sketching, photographing, mapping — were merely a cover for gathering information that might be useful to a foreign power. If there were any truth to these rumours, thought Ezra, perhaps his dream of murder might not be so far-fetched after all.

The Forrester letters that Vasco, the vineyard manager, had found in the dovecot might prove to be very interesting.

Ezra took out the envelope Sykes had given him and withdrew the two sheets of paper inside. The letterhead bore the company crest embossed in blue. On the left was a column of names, to the right remarks about their duties and when they had been hired.

The first name was Vasco Gedes. He had succeeded his father as vineyard

40

manager and had held the position for eighteen years. Apart from his responsibilities in the vineyard he was Matthew Sykes' occasional chauffeur. 'Can fix the Mercedes with a hairpin,' was the remark against his name, followed by, 'little English.'

Ezra continued reading.

Gertrudes Figueira, cook (excellent!). Twelve years' service. Can understand more than she makes out.

Anna Figueira, daughter of Gertrudes. Seventeen or eighteen. Wears false teeth. Waits at table, occasional chambermaid. Speaks more English than her mother.

Maria Theresa Figueira, Gertrudes' sister. Chambermaid. Clumsy. No English. Eight years' service.

Albino Sousa, farm manager. Liaison with harvesters, vineyard workers. Only 10 per cent hearing. Handy when dealing with workers' complaints. Third generation at Santo Pedro.

Francisco Ribeira, gardener. Eleven years' service. Blind in left eye. No English . . .

Ezra smiled to himself. It seemed that Matthew Sykes' quinta was a haven for the physically disadvantaged.

* * *

The train had passed the Régua dam and the village of Bagauste. Vineyards rose from the water on both banks in a series of graduated steps defined by low walls to a line of olive trees. The symmetry of the vines in regimented rows contrasted strangely with the wild ruggedness of the terrain around them. The scudding clouds passing the sun caused moving shadows to play on the outcrops of granite too dense and primordial to be reclaimed as vineyard land.

At Ferrao the slopes became more dramatic and as the train came within sight of the Pinhão bridge, Ezra could see on the south side of the river the brown bosom of the mountain swelling above the treeline, traversed by dusty grey roads. Clusters of white houses with red-tiled roofs dotted the mountain. As the train pulled into the town of Pinhão Ezra could see the port lodges belonging to Ferreira and then Calem.

Even in the late afternoon the heat was intense as he stepped down onto the platform, suitcase in hand. He put on a pair of sunglasses to cut the glare. As he walked into the station hall he glanced around for Vasco and the Mercedes he could fix with a hairpin.

It always amused Ezra, when he stepped out of customs at airports, to see the rows of drivers holding cards with names printed on them to identify their clients. He wondered if Sykes' part-time chauffeur would be there with a card. Not that there was any need. At his height and size he could not be mistaken for a Portuguese and there were few people on the train.

Inside Pinhão's station hall Ezra was distracted by the marvellous tiled images of the grape harvest and port production that decorated its walls. Executed in blue and white, each scene was minutely detailed and elaborately framed with painted scrolls and devices in yellow gold. He paused in front of one panel representing the loading of the traditional *barco rabelo* with pipes of port for their journey down the Douro to Vila Nova de Gaia. He had not noticed before how similar these boats were to Viking warships. He recalled a scrap of information he had read somewhere that before 1792 these flat-hulled craft were built to carry up to one hundred barrels. The casks were never completely filled so that, in the case of disaster on the difficult journey through the cataracts, they would float and their precious contents would not be lost.

He stepped out into the dusty street and looked around for Vasco.

Across the road, parked in the shade of a horse chestnut tree, was a 1995 cream-coloured Mercedes E-320 Cabriolet convertible, its top down. Leaning against it was a woman dressed in powder blue slacks and a sleeveless white blouse. She wore a large straw hat that kept the sun from her face and hid her hair. Her legs were crossed at the ankles, her feet in expensive Italian sandals. Her right arm was bent across her waist supporting the elbow of her left arm which stood dramatically upright, tapering to long, slim fingers that ended in a cigarette. She was looking down towards the river, her face in half-profile to him.

Ezra was struck by the way she held herself and wondered if she was as beautiful behind her sunglasses and shaded face as the picture she presented. He moved towards her, delighted that Maria, the housekeeper, would be his companion up to the quinta rather than Vasco of the 'little English'.

'Good afternoon,' he said as he approached.

The woman turned to him, dropped the cigarette to the road and lowered her sunglasses.

Her eyes were blue-green, the colour of the Atlantic Ocean on a sunny day. She placed her palms on the door behind her. Ezra noted the gold ring on her left hand. He judged her to be in her late thirties.

She was slim and bronzed and well cared for.

'You don't look like a photographer,' she said, in fluent but accented English.

'I'm a writer, not a photographer.'

Ezra travelled with a battered old Nikon and was competent enough to take shots acceptable to most of the magazines to which he contributed.

'Shall I put this in the back seat or would you like it in the boot?' he asked, holding his suitcase in front of him.

The woman frowned and did not move. She seemed to be staring over his shoulder. Ezra heard the sound of a van draw up behind him.

'Katarina Soares?'

A man's voice. The woman levered herself away from the car and brushed past him. Ezra turned.

He saw a van parked outside the entrance to the station, so dusty that he could not tell its original colour. The motor was idling and the acrid smell of burning oil rose from its rattling exhaust pipe.

The woman conferred with the unseen

driver and looked back at Ezra. Then she returned to his side and smiled at him.

'You must forgive me. There has been a mistake. This is the gentleman I am waiting for.'

Ezra could feel himself redden in embarrassment. To cover his confusion he opened the door of the Mercedes for her.

'Then it's my loss,' he said.

As she slid gracefully into the driver's seat Ezra heard the unmistakable sound of a camera shutter on speed wind. He turned in the direction of the sound and he saw the van driver's face for the first time. He was positive he had seen it before. Very recently in fact. On the quay under the Dom Luis I Bridge not three hours ago.

The woman in the Mercedes pulled away from the kerb and the van followed her. The plates were obscured with mud but Ezra was struck by the width of the back tyres, a twin set custom-fitted to carry a greater than normal load. Sufficient, he thought, for transporting many cases of wine or a mobile studio with camera equipment.

★ ★ ★

Vasco arrived ten minutes later driving a 1971 Mercedes 300SEL. He jumped out of the car and held the door to the passenger seat open. On the back seat, lying on an old newspaper, was a rooster. Vasco smiled and drove his fist into the palm of his hand, miming the bird's fate. The eloquent shrug that followed spoke volumes: there was no point in wasting a perfectly good fowl but he did not want to mess the back seat so he had to find a newspaper. Hence he was delayed.

'Excuse, please, excuse, please,' Vasco kept saying as he ushered Ezra into the car.

He was a small man, dark with a large head and a gold tooth that flashed in the sun whenever he smiled. He wore a blue shirt and faded, tight-fitting jeans.

'Are Mercedes standard issue in the port trade?' asked Ezra as he settled into the front seat.

'Please?'

'I saw another Mercedes. I thought it belonged to Mr Sykes.'

48

'Mercedes. Mr Sykes, yes,' said Vasco, slapping the steering wheel with pride.

Ezra tried another approach.

'A Mercedes with no roof.'

He raised his hands above his head and mimed a convertible.

Again Vasco nodded and slapped the roof.

Ezra sat back and looked out of the window. They had left the town and were climbing up a dusty road. The rows of vines on their narrow terraces looked like corn-braiding across the brow of the hills. Clusters of plump berries black as night hung from the canes above the stony soil awaiting the knives of the harvesters. The hills folded into each other only to rise again in ever paler shades of green and purple, stretching to a distant horizon. Though men had shaped this unforgiving landscape over the centuries it still had the look of a cosmic frown, savage and brooding in its ominous silence.

Here and there Ezra could see patches of colour moving through the vines. Men and women in blue caps and head-scarves performing the annual ritual of bringing home the harvest. He watched their slow procession along the rows. Men bent under the weight of large, square wicker baskets, they call *gigos*, piled high with grapes. They balanced them precariously on the napes of their necks, anchored to their shoulders by a strap secured around their foreheads. On their heads they wore a cowl-like sack of hessian that protected their necks from the sun and the chafing effect of their burden. But these were small, wiry men, going about their business heads bowed, chin touching their chest in an attitude of prayer.

They were driving due east from the town of Pinhão, climbing and then dipping into valleys before climbing ever higher. Vasco drove slowly, taking exaggerated caution at each hairpin bend as if he had been instructed by his employer not to alarm the guest.

The sudden appearance of a grouping of red-tiled roofs denoted another quinta. There was no order here as in most wine regions Ezra had visited, no clear-cut division between one man's property and his neighbour's.

'Quinta do Santo Pedro,' said Vasco, dipping his head almost beneath the dashboard and pointing up the steep slope.

'Can we stop? I'd like to take a photo.'

Ezra mimed his intention and Vasco drew the car into the side of the road that had now become a rutted track. Before he knew it, Vasco had opened his door and was waiting for him to step out.

He stood in the shade of a wild olive tree, his Nikon slung around his neck. Far below was the river reflecting the undulating curves of the land. Above him, climbing in a series of wide steps, were rows of vines right up to the farmhouse and its surrounding buildings. There were more vineyards stretching above the dazzling white walls of the quinta almost to the summit where the last rays of the evening sun glinted off stainless steel tanks partially obscured by a row of cypress trees at the top.

He pointed enquiringly at the tanks and the man shook his head, scowling.

'Quinta do Coteiro.'

Vasco tapped his index fingers together

and spat on the ground.

Ezra looked through his viewfinder and began to focus his telescopic lens on his host's property. He could see a plume of smoke rising from the house.

Odd, he thought, it was too early to be cooking dinner and there was no need to warm the house in the September heat.

He clicked the shutter and raised the lens to the top of the hill. He could not see the farm buildings behind the cypress trees, before he saw a cloud of dust on a track that ran along the eastern edge of Matthew Sykes' vineyard. Beyond it was land that lay fallow, recently dug and prepared to receive vines. He trained his telescopic lens on the vehicle. It was the same van he had seen outside the station. Even with the magnification of the lens he could not make out the driver.

'*Vengo*,' said Vasco, plucking at the sleeve of his jacket.

They drew up to a pair of white iron gates, surmounted by a small bell set onto the lintel in its own tiny concrete arch. The gates shielded the house from view. Ezra could see a wave of grey smoke pouring over the whitewashed walls. From behind them he could hear the sound of water under pressure, the squeak of rubber boots on flagstones and the barking of commands in Portuguese.

Vasco, muttering to himself, ran around to open the door for Ezra who was already half out of the car.

'Leave it,' said Ezra as Vasco went to unlock the boot for his suitcase. 'Later.'

Vasco slipped a key into the lock and opened the gate. Across a small court-yard, attached to the two-storey farm house, stood a small baroque chapel with a plaster coat of arms above its ornate wooden door. Smoke was billowing from one of its windows. Men in blue overalls rushed to the source of the smoke and threw buckets of water at the wall. In the centre stood a tall young man in shorts and hobnailed boots holding a green garden hose directed through one of the blackened windows. He was shouting at the workers and even though Ezra spoke no Portuguese he could tell the words fell on their backs like lashes.

Luke, thought Ezra.

'Can I help?'

The young man turned.

'You must be Mr Brant. I'm sorry about this. Spot of bother but everything's under control.'

The ingratiating charm suddenly disappeared as Luke switched to Portuguese and began to berate Vasco. Then his face relaxed once more and he was smiling again.

'Silly bugger. Wouldn't have got to this if he'd been back here when he should have.'

'What happened?'

'Freakish really. Someone left a glass of water on one of the pews. Must have acted like a magnifying glass. Burnt through the wood and set the bloody thing alight. Dad's going to go bonkers when he sees it. Hello, I'm Luke, by the way.'

'Ezra.'

He had his father's eyes and sunken cheekbones.

'I'll get Vasco to show you to your room. You'll probably want to freshen up. Why don't you meet me here in an hour, we'll have a drink and I'll give you the tour? They're pressing tonight. Tourists love it.'

'Then I'm sure I shall too,' remarked Ezra, feeling as if he had been patronized.

Oblivious, Luke shouted at Vasco who scuttled out of the gate to fetch Ezra's suitcase.

'We usually dine about eight. Hope you like tripe. Gertrudes, our cook, has prepared the local delicacy, *tripas à moda do Porto*. Can't stand it myself.'

'But tourists love it.'

Luke smiled and ran a wet hand through his abundant black hair. Vasco returned with the suitcase and after another verbal onslaught from Luke he led Ezra across the courtyard past the orange trees and a small ornamental fountain.

The covered verandah with its coconut matting was defined by neatly clipped yew bushes that grew out of coffin-like boxes painted green. A large eucalyptus tree dominated the house from the back and dropped its leaves on the red-tiled roof. The shuttered windows of the upstairs rooms facing the river were shaded by the overhanging eaves. The depth of the eaves created a shaded balcony enclosed within wrought iron railings painted the same colour as the boxes below.

The wire-mesh door banged behind him as Ezra followed Vasco inside. The spacious hallway was cool and airy. Beside the door was a large wooden coat rack festooned with straw hats of all shapes and sizes. Next to it stood an elephant's foot bristling with walking sticks, canes and umbrellas. To his right was the living room that looked as if it had been imported from an English country house — overstuffed sofas and chairs in fading floral fabric. Every possible surface was covered with bric-à-brac, Toby jugs, wooden boxes, paper-weights and old tobacco jars. In one corner stood a vintage rocking horse missing its tail. Botanical watercolours of grapes, flowers and vegetables decorated the walls. There were English magazines in cane holders by each chair and boxes of games Ezra hadn't played since he was a child stacked on shelves beside the fireplace.

The staircase in front of him was hung with old family photos, a young Matthew Sykes with his father and uncle presiding over the harvest, Matthew draped over a 1956 Sunbeam Alpine, Matthew playing cricket, croquet, waving from a launch on the Douro. But there were no photos with his wife and none of Luke.

Vasco led him down the corridor, past a grandfather clock, and opened a door. The room smelled of pot-pourri. The double bed was covered with a Laura Ashley counterpane. Next to it was a washstand complete with water pitcher and bowl. There was a writing table and a chair and what looked like an old valve radio. The walls were hung with hunting prints. The blinds were drawn across the windows and instinctively Ezra crossed to open them. The floorboards creaked under his weight. He threw back the curtains, opened the window and pushed back the shutters. The window gave out onto the back of the property where a line of ilex bushes appeared to separate

Quinta do Santo Pedro from its neighbour above.

The smell of French lavender, the white-petalled gum cistus and wood smoke filled his nostrils. In the warm sweet air a hawk wheeled on the currents, a black speck against the clouds.

Vasco placed his suitcase on the bed and showed him where the bathroom was down the hall. He returned to his bedroom, pleased to be alone at last. He opened his suitcase and began to hang up his clothes in the large wooden wardrobe that smelled of camphor.

Ezra wondered if the fire had started accidentally as Luke had suggested or whether it was part of the campaign of intimidation his father had asked him to investigate. Did Luke know that his father had taken him into his confidence, or was Matthew Sykes maybe withholding information from his son?

A knock at the door interrupted these speculations.

'Come in.'

The door opened and in came a woman in her early forties.

'Hello, My name is Helen. I'm the chatelaine. Actually, I'm Matthew Sykes' niece. Welcome to Santo Pedro.'

There was something vaguely apologetic in the way she introduced herself as if she were awed by the responsibility with which she had been entrusted. She held out her hand while clutching a pile of towels to her breast. The fingers were red and swollen as if she had just removed them from hot water. Her ring finger had an indentation as if she had removed the band while she was washing and had forgotten to put it on again.

'Thank you. I'm Ezra Brant. It's beautiful here.'

'You wouldn't say that if you had to spend a winter up here.'

She was a tall woman who might have been beautiful but for the length of her face. The bony nose seemed to run in the family. She wore a long, loose-fitting dress and sandals. Her hair was pulled back from her face and plaited in a single, long braid that fell to her waist.

'You arrived to some excitement.'

'Yes.'

59

'And you met my cousin Luke?'

'Yes.'

'I've brought you some towels. Oh, and this envelope. Matthew phoned and asked me to give it to you when you arrived.'

'Thank you. Did Mr Sykes say when he would be here?'

'He can't make it tonight in time for dinner so I imagine he'll stay at his club and drive up in the morning. He seems to be spending less time here now that Luke is managing the quinta,' said Helen, as if she was talking to herself.

'And Mrs Sykes, will she be here for dinner?'

Ezra knew full well that Amanda Sykes would not be setting foot on the quinta grounds but he wanted to hear what Helen might say about her uncle's marital situation.

'Aunt Amanda sends her regrets but she can't make it tonight.'

'I imagine I'll see her during the celebrations then.'

'I'll just leave these towels on the dresser for you. If you need anything just call.'

'I'm looking forward to crushing,' said Ezra, attempting to keep the conversation going. 'All the years I've been writing about wine, I've never got my feet into the vat.'

'It's a messy business. I did it once,' said Helen, 'I broke out in hives.'

It occurred to Ezra that Matthew Sykes had not included Helen on his list of those who worked at the quinta. In fact, all the names on the list were Portuguese. Helen was family but she introduced herself as the chatelaine, the keeper of the keys.

When she left Ezra sat on the bed and opened the envelope she had handed to him. It contained an oilskin pouch tied with twine. He undid the twine and opened it. Inside was a bundle of letters in their original envelopes and some browning sheets of paper that looked as if they were drafts or copies of letters that had been sent. Ezra shuffled through the envelopes. They were penned in black ink, each letter printed rather than linked in sloping italics, as if written to a child or to someone whose first language was not

English. Several of the envelopes were addressed to Dona Antonia Adelaide Ferreira at Quinta das Nogueiras and one to her at a country estate in Brentwood, Essex.

The letters appeared to have been placed in chronological order and Ezra was careful not to disturb the sequence. He withdrew the letter from the first envelope, opened the page and glanced at the signature on the bottom: 'Your most faithful and respectful friend, Joseph James Forrester, Vila Nova de Gaia, 24th February, 1853.'

With mounting excitement he began to read.

My dear Dona Antonia, It is with a heavy heart I must impart some intelligence that affects you and your family. I urge you to act expeditiously in this matter once I have apprised you of the situation. You will recall that two years ago I was commissioned to paint a second portrait of your Prime Minister, the Duke of Saldanha. The canvas was damaged slightly by an unknown vandal and the Duke called me in, requesting that I make such repairs as I deemed necessary. I asked that the portrait be delivered to my house in Vila Nova de Gaia so that I could work on it in my studio. The aide who transported it there was a loose-tongued fellow who mentioned that the Duke was anxious to have the portrait restored to its habitual place in time for the marriage of his son. Since there had been no report of the imminent nuptials in the Court Circular I questioned the fellow as to who was the prospective bride. It was only after oiling his tongue with a bottle of Kopke's 1834 that I learned the sad facts I am communicating in haste to you now. It appears that the Duke is intent upon marrying his son to your daughter, Maria da Assunçao, notwithstanding that she is but eleven years of age. (No doubt he has cast a covetous eye on your estates in the Douro which he expects to be part of her dowry.)

Such is his determination in this matter, according to my intoxicated informant, that he is prepared to have Maria kidnapped and brought to the altar by force if you refuse her hand. A platoon of his personal guards has been organized to escort Maria to Lisbon if his overtures to you are rebuffed. My informant told me that, as an inducement, the Duke would bestow upon you the title of Condessa de Vesúvio. As you know from your country's painful history during the Civil War the Duke of Saldanha is not a man given to compromise or negotiation. For your own safety and that of your daughter I strongly urge you to absent yourself from Portugal at this time. I have friends in England who would gladly open their houses to a lady of your nobility and charm. I would deem it an honour to make the necessary arrangements for you. In the meantime, I respectfully suggest that you and your daughter absent yourself immediately from the Casa de

Travassos and take refuge in the Convento das Chagas at Lemego. The Mother Superior, Sister Angelica, is a trusted friend whose loyalty is matched only by her discretion. I will be in contact with you there . . .

Ezra gave a low whistle. Why was Forrester writing to Dona Antonia, the richest woman in Portugal (her Quinta do Vale de Meao estate alone was valued at $6 million) and not to her second husband, Francisco José da Silva Torres? Torres was the manager of her estates whom she had married on the death of her first husband, Antonio Bernardo Ferreira II, who was also her cousin. Ezra had read that Antonio, unlike his shy and retiring wife, enjoyed a good party and entertained lavishly but he had died in 1844. Was the second marriage one of mere convenience, a decision by a pragmatic woman to share her bed with a man so that the family estates would be well run and her manager would not be robbing her blind? And was Forrester's concern for the dour Dona Antonia more than that of a friend? His own wife had died in 1847 and his six children had been left behind in England to be cared for by relatives and friends. He lived without female companionship in a household that consisted of a butler, a housekeeper, a groom and a general factotum/bodyguard named Francisco.

The letter from Forrester to Dona Antonia in Brentford, Essex, franked two months later, suggested that he had made good on his offer and that Maria and her mother had fled to England to escape the threat of enforced matrimony. Ezra was about to read it when there was another knock on the door.

'Ezra?'

Luke's voice. Ezra's instinctive reaction was to throw his jacket over the letters on the bed to conceal the fact that he had them.

'Come in, it's open.'

'This fax just arrived for you from my father. Why would you want the guest list?' he smiled. 'Do you write a gossip column too?'

'No, I'm just choosy about the

company I keep,' replied Ezra.

There was something about the young man's arrogant self-possession that annoyed him.

'It's all set up in the courtyard so I'll see you down there when you're ready.'

Luke closed the door before Ezra had a chance to respond. He wondered how a man as charming and concerned as Matthew Sykes could have such a truculent son.

He shook his head and spread the three-page fax out on the bed cover. Sykes had added a short handwritten note to the top of what looked like a secretary's mailing list. 'Here is the list, Ezra. The Government guests are marked with an asterisk. Anything you need for your book, just ask. M.S.'

Also attached was one sheet headed 'Programme of Events.'

He scanned the list of names. Many he recognized from the port trade, fellow shippers with English and Dutch names: James and Peter Symington, Peter Cobb, Alistair Robertson, Bruce Guimarens,

Dirk Niepoort. There were several Sykes, members of the family who would be flying in from England for the occasion. The only Portuguese names appeared to be bankers from Lisbon and Oporto, the local mayor and the priest. Except for that of Alvaro Soares and on the original copy Sykes had put a question mark against it.

★　★　★

Walking down the staircase Ezra's nostrils were assailed by an aroma he had never smelled before. A mix of beef, spicy bacon and cumin. So heady and inviting was the scent that it made him salivate and drew him to the whitewashed kitchen from where it emanated.

A large woman in a floral overall and bedroom slippers was standing on the flagstones in front of an old-fashioned wood-burning stove, leaning over a huge pot. She held a wooden spoon in both hands and was stirring the concoction inside. The rising steam was fogging up her glasses and dampening her grey hair that was swept back from her forehead and held by a plastic comb in the shape of a peacock.

Along one wall was an open cabinet with the aluminium cooking pots set neatly in rows, glistening with droplets of water. The severe line of the shelves had been softened with pelmets of lace that had been thumb-tacked into the wood.

Ezra breathed in deeply to announce his presence. The woman turned and drew one enormous arm across her forehead then wiped her hands on a dish towel hanging from her waist.

'You must be Gertrudes.'

The woman nodded solemnly.

'That smells absolutely delicious,' he said. 'What is it?'

Gertrudes' face erupted into a smile, causing the rolls of fat around her neck to jiggle along with her dangling golden earrings.

'*Tripas à moda do Porto*,' she beamed and she withdrew the wooden spoon and offered him a taste.

'Mmmm, wonderful. My name is Ezra. I come from Canada.'

'Toronto?'

'You know Toronto?'

'I have cousin in Toronto.'

Wherever Ezra travelled invariably he came across someone who had a cousin in Toronto. There was a large and flourishing Portuguese community in Toronto and many good Portuguese restaurants.

'He work at Chiado.'

'I know Chiado's. I've eaten there many times.'

'He cooks.'

'And I bet you taught him everything you know.'

Gertrudes smiled again and cocked her head bashfully to one side. Ezra took out his notebook.

'Tell me, how do you make *Tripas à moda do Porto*?

Gertrudes beckoned him closer to the stove. She plunged her wooden spoon in and withdrew a heaped serving.

'*Tripas*,' she said, pointing to the calf's tripe.

Ezra began to write in a hand that only he could decipher. The language could have been in code because not even his ex-wife could read his handwriting, just as he could never read his father's. Although he had no excuse since he wasn't a doctor.

'Leg of the calf.'

Gertrudes introduced each ingredient with a flourish. 'Chouriço sausage, pig's ear, bacon, head of the pig, chicken, beans, carrots, onions, parsley, bayleaf, cumin, salt, pepper, *salamagundi*. All in the pot.'

'What is *salamagundi*?' he asked.

Gertrudes took him by the arm and led him to the butcher's block table in the centre of the kitchen. She pointed to a large metal bowl. It contained a salad of chopped-up cold meat, raw vegetables, boiled eggs, pickles and anchovies.

'*Salamagundi*.'

'Ahh,' said Ezra.

'Drinks before dinner.'

The grating voice of Luke from the kitchen doorway.

'You mustn't miss the view from the terrace at this time. You should bring your camera, the light is perfect.'

'I'm just coming,' said Ezra.

A table set with a blindingly white tablecloth had been set next to the ornamental fountain. A bottle of white port stood next to a bottle of twelve-year-old Macallan malt whisky, a soda syphon, a chromium-plated ice bucket and two Waterford crystal scotch glasses.

'I've taken the liberty of pouring you a glass of white port. With a lemon peel to cut the sweetness. And some ice,' said Luke, handing him a glass as he eased himself into the canvas deckchair.

'Do you spend the whole year here?' asked Ezra, breaking the silence between them. Luke had been gazing abstractedly towards the setting sun, his whisky glass held by the rim between thumb and forefinger. Ezra noticed a long scar across the base of his thumb that disappeared under his watch strap.

'Yes, twelve months a year.'

'Don't you ever miss London?'

'London? Whatever for? I was born here. This is my home.'

'But you have family there. Your father is in England quite a bit.'

Luke flicked the hair out of his eyes and took a sip of his drink.

'My father leaves the running of the quinta to me. He takes care of the export side and the financial aspects of the business. Dealing with the Shylocks, that sort of thing.'

Ezra felt uncomfortable with the expression. His own mother had been Jewish and he could sense in the young man that strain of well-bred anti-Semitism that persisted in a certain type of Englishman. He decided to change the subject.

'How do you see the future of Quinta do Santo Pedro then?'

'Is this an interview?'

'Let's just say it could become part of the piece I'm going to write. So, let's make it on the record,' said Ezra, taking out his notebook.

'Fire away.'

'We were talking about the future.'

'The future,' said Luke, staring out across the river. 'I've been trying to convince my father we should invest in some cellars up here instead of trucking our wines down to Vila Nova de Gaia. Quinta do Noval is doing it. They've built a huge cellar down there near Pinhão and they're even going to bottle there. If we were to do it it would save us a lot of money in the end and our quality would be better. God knows what those tanker lorries do to the wines, sloshing around on those mountain roads, getting bruised. All you need is for one shipment to be polluted and you're finished.'

'What do you mean, polluted?'

'Simple. The slightest bacteria in one of those tankers and you've lost your harvest. Then you could get sabotaged.'

'Sabotaged?'

'A competitor. A fellow pays off the driver, a little diesel fuel finds its way into the tank and bingo!'

'And I thought port was a gentleman's business,' said Ezra.

'The valley is changing. The traditional ways won't work any more,' said Luke, shielding his eyes from the last rays of the sun as it died behind the browning stubble of the cornfields across the river.

'I believe the future of this quinta is in

red wine. Table wine that doesn't take fifteen years to soften up in the bottle.'

'You'd give up port production?'

'No, not entirely. I'm saying we should shift our emphasis to what the market wants. Red wine. Have you ever tasted Barca Velha?'

'Yes, the Ferreira company put on a vertical tasting of Barca Velha going back to the 60s for me last time I was in Oporto.'

'That's what I want to make. A Portuguese wine that rivals Château Latour. But I need new equipment to do it. Rotary fermenters, double-jacketed tanks. New French barrels. My father has an exaggerated sense of charity, Mr Brant. Quinta do Santo Pedro has become a charity ward for the halt, the lame and the blind. Instead of installing indoor plumbing for the workers he should be getting rid of the terraces to make one large sloping vineyard and putting money into stainless steel tanks.'

'You mean you want to get rid of the lagares?'

'Crushing by foot will be as dead as the

dodo in a few years. The young Portuguese guys aren't interested in following in their fathers' footsteps, if you'll pardon the pun. They watch too much American television. And they see their fathers and uncles working twelve hours a day in the vine-yards and then coming back here to spend another four hours to stomp grapes. And what for? A few miserable escudos. They're just not going to do it. Sure, it all looks very romantic.'

The report of a distant shotgun prompted them both to look back up the hill. The double blast echoed across the valley.

'What are they hunting?'

'Wild boar. Sometimes wolves.'

Ezra's gaze settled on the stainless steel tanks on the crest of the hill.

'Tell me about the quinta up there.'

'Coteiro? It's owned by a Portuguese. They specialize in tawny ports. Some of them are quite good, the twenty-year-old particularly. Their land is well-drained. They have about 300 hectares here and directly across the river. That plot just below the cornfield. They could make very good vintage port if they tried.'

'Do you buy grapes from them?'

'Not bloody likely.'

The vehemence with which Luke uttered the statement surprised Ezra. It seemed there was no love lost between the two neighbours.

'Those tanks are a bit of an eyesore,' he said.

'At least they have them,' grumbled Luke.

'I remember when Taylor's painted a huge green sign in their vineyard advertising their name. There was a hell of an outcry,' said Ezra.

'The Portuguese seem to be able to get away with these things. British firms have to be more circumspect. We've been here three hundred years but they still look on us as visitors. He has a helipad up there too, you know. Behind the line of trees.'

'You're kidding.'

'He uses it to spray his vineyards. It drives my father bonkers. If Dad had his way he'd mount a bazooka on the roof.'

'What's his name?'

'Alvaro Soares.'

Ezra nodded. The question mark against the name made sense now. Matthew Sykes was unsure as to whether he should invite his neighbour to the bicentennial celebration of the quinta or ignore him.

'Is he any relation to Katarina Soares?'

'How do you know Katarina Soares?' asked Luke, genuinely surprised and somewhat offended.

'I don't. I ran into her at the railway station when I arrived. I thought she'd come to pick me up.'

Luke studied a column of black ants as they negotiated their way through the loose gravel of the courtyard.

'Katarina is Alvaro Soares' wife.'

He rose from his chair and put his glass on the table.

'Come. I'll show you the lagar. The men are crushing now.'

★ ★ ★

The rectangular lagar, an open tank with metre-high granite walls, rather like a toddler's paddling pool, was located in a barn at the back of the house. It was broad enough to accommodate the nine men who were standing in a line, up to their knees in grape must, with their arms over each other's shoulders. They were dressed in blue shorts and red plaid shirts. The men at both ends of the line held wooden staves which they used as walking sticks outside the tank to help them balance themselves. One of them shouted the time as they marched slowly up and down the tank, their thighs stained purple.

The sound of the leader's voice and the ringing strike of the staves on the stone step around the lagar rose through the whitewashed beams above their heads and bounced off the roof. There was a military precision about the men's work. The movement of their legs in a sea of purple, already frothing as the fermentation commenced, caused small waves to lap against the granite walls of the lagar.

Ezra was fascinated by the sight. He felt he had stepped back in time. When man first learned how to ferment grape juice he extracted it by crushing the berries under foot. God gave us feet, Ezra was convinced, so that we could make wine because the foot is the ideal tool for this purpose. It has sufficient power to crush a berry and press out its juice, at the same time extracting colouring matter from the skins; but the sole has enough elasticity to avoid crushing the pits and stalks that would impart astringent, bitter tannins to the wine.

'Is there a set number of men for treading?'

'For the *corta*, the first crushing, it's usually two men per pipe of port. A pipe is 534 litres which equals 252 *canadas*.'

'Canadas?'

'Thought that would amuse you. A canada is a measure of 2.1 litres. The Portuguese are very pragmatic. They reckon that a canada is the most a man could drink.'

'Two point one litres. That's nearly three bottles.'

'Give or take a hangover or two. They'll be taking a break in a moment,' said Luke, consulting his watch. 'Their first two-hour shift is almost up.'

As he spoke Ezra could hear the sound of an approaching accordionist and the flute-like notes of women laughing. Suddenly, at a signal from their leader, the treaders broke rank and began to walk around the larger, hands behind their backs, singing.

'It's a traditional song called 'Liberdade,' ' explained Luke.

'What does it mean?'

'Liberty, ah liberty, Only to the few you're known. If only I had liberty just to call my feet my own.'

The women, dressed in shorts and blouses, passed small glasses of *bagaceira*, Portugal's fiery eau-de-vie, to their menfolk. They handed round cigarettes and then jumped into the lagar themselves.

'Why don't you have a bash?' asked Luke.

Ezra needed no second invitation. He had put his swimming trunks on under his trousers following Luke's instructions and was ready for action. He slipped off his shoes and socks and to the amusement of the women who were dancing and singing in the lagar he removed his trousers. In his white short-sleeved shirt tight across his paunch and his boxer trunks he looked like a middle-aged wrestler gone to seed. Gingerly, he placed one leg over the granite ledge and lowered it into the soupy mass. It was slightly warm and scratchy from the grape stems, rather like wading through half-cooked porridge.

The men and women who were not dancing with each other moved around the edges of the lagar with their arms folded. A rotund woman with closely cropped grey hair said something in Portuguese and everybody including Luke guffawed with laughter. She approached Ezra with her hands on her hips and looked up at him, winking. One of her front teeth was missing. She held out her hands and took his. Oh my God, he thought, she wants to dance.

At the best of times, under the best of circumstances, Ezra was no dancer. He had danced at his wedding and once at a staff Christmas party at the *Toronto*

Examiner but he could not remember any other occasion. The old woman began to gyrate and hum tunelessly through her nose as the accordionist moved closer. The other treaders stopped and moved into a circle around them, clapping in time, cigarettes dangling from mouths.

The only face that was not smiling was a swarthy man who had been calling out the time for the marching men. He sat on the edge of the lagar scowling, his arms folded across his chest.

Ezra, his hands clasped tightly by his dancing partner, lifted his feet like a circus elephant and coloured as red as the liquid that lapped around his knees.

The woman pirouetted under his outstretched arm, strutted and batted her eyelids coquettishly at him, much to the delight of the bystanders. Ezra's white shirt was splashed with juice. He could feel the stalks catching between his toes. The smell of the sweet fruit made him feel nauseous. He wanted out.

He let go of the woman's hand and she began to fall backwards. Luckily, there were hands to catch her and Ezra beat his retreat to the edge of the lagar and sat down.

As he sat trying to catch his breath his toe struck something hard and circular on the bottom of the lagar. It felt like a ring. He tried to manoeuvre it between his toes so that he could pick it up. Eventually he succeeded and when he raised his foot he saw that he had retrieved a gold wedding band.

The scowling man had witnessed his furtive movements.

Ezra slipped the ring quickly into his swimming trunks as Luke approached, applauding.

'Bravo, Mr Brant. Capital. We'll have to put you on the payroll.'

'I just hope you declare a vintage year so I can say I had a foot in it,' said Ezra, as he swung his legs over the wall.

The scowling man waded quickly over to where he stood and grabbed him by the shoulders, shouting at him over the din of the music. Instinctively, Ezra wheeled around to break the man's grip, raising his arms to protect his face. The movement caused the man to stumble and fall backwards into the sea of liquid skins. He struggled to his knees, cursing, amidst the barely hidden smirks of his fellow workers.

'I'm sorry,' said Ezra, as the man thrashed blindly in the must, trying to regain his footing. 'Truly, I'm sorry.'

Soaked through his shirt and shorts the man pulled himself up on the lagar wall, his face a mask of fury. He locked his eyes on Ezra and slowly, very deliberately, he began to run his hands down his legs to channel the juice back into the lagar.

'That's what he was trying to tell you,' laughed Luke. 'It's customary to leave as much juice behind as you can.'

Ezra heaved himself up onto the wall and imitated the man's actions. He watched the droplets of purple juice caught on the hairs of his legs as they ran through his fingers and down his calves. The man continued to stare maniacally at him.

Once Ezra had removed as much juice as he could he approached the man who was still standing on the lagar wall, legs apart, fists on his hips.

'I really do apologize, I didn't mean to do that,' he said.

The man continued to glower down at him.

'He doesn't speak English,' whispered Luke, who appeared to be enjoying the scene.

'Can you translate for me?'

Luke said something in Portuguese which did not seem to mollify the man. His anger only grew as he caught those around him laughing behind their hands. The object of this ill-concealed derision bit into the palm of his hand and jumped off the wall, walking to the door with as much dignity as he could muster.

'What was all that about?' Ezra asked Luke, as he washed the stains from his legs under the tap at the far end of the barn.

'That's Albino Sousa, our farm manager. He's very protective of our port. Doesn't like tourists, doesn't like foreigners in general. He once went to Oporto about ten years ago, hated it and has never left the valley since.'

'Charming,' said Ezra. 'What happens to the wine now?'

'We leave it overnight to settle and tomorrow a smaller group will come in and tread to stir up the must until we have the desired amount of unfermented sugar. Then we open the lagar and run off the juice into the vats.'

'And you fortify at that point?'

'Yes. Little by little we add brandy of a strength of between 76 and 78 degrees alcohol.'

'How much brandy will you add?'

'One hundred litres for every 450 litres of must. Dinner is at eight thirty,' said Luke, handing him a towel, impatient to move.

Ezra watched him leave. The accordionist seemed to play with more gusto after Luke's departure and the treaders, no longer under the gaze of their employer, began to dance and sing with spontaneous abandon.

Ezra put his trousers back on and before zipping up his fly he reached inside his trunks for the ring.

In the privacy of his room he studied it

under the bedside light. The gold was scratched and dull. He tried it on his little finger but it would not fit. Most likely a woman's ring, he thought. Inside was a two-word inscription, now barely legible: it read, 'Undying Love'.

★   ★   ★

The tripe had been delicious at dinner but now it sat on Ezra's stomach like the calf who had surrendered its own for his delectation and delight. He had eaten by himself in the dining room at the highly polished Chippendale table. Luke Sykes had left a note propped up against the port decanter apologizing for not being able to join him. He offered some vague excuse about a sudden emergency he had to deal with.

Ezra wondered if it was another 'incident' calculated to disrupt the approaching celebration.

He had heard the phone ring while he was showering and a few moments later the slamming of the screen door followed by the creak of the metal gates. From his window he saw the headlights of a jeep pulling out of the property and disappearing down the road dragging a tunnel of dust behind it.

He had sat alone at the long family table, served by young Anna Figueira whose false teeth clicked with every step she took.

'How long have you been working here?' he had asked her.

'Please?'

'How many years are you working at the quinta?'

He enunciated the words clearly and slowly.

The girl blushed and held up three fingers.

'Do you like it here?'

The girl looked nervously at the door to the kitchen and then back at Ezra.

'Is it a good life in Canada?' she asked.

There were tears in her eyes and Ezra noticed that there was bruising on her upper arms.

★   ★   ★

He washed his meal down with a few glasses of Quinta do Cotto Grande Escolha 1990. It was concentrated and jammy, too rich and dense a table wine for the tripe dish, but very satisfying as the cool breezes from the mountains blew through the open window. He refused coffee which kept him awake, poured himself a glass of port and took it up to his bedroom.

In the tomb-like silence of his room he took out a file of notes from his suitcase, opened his computer and began to work on his book, knowing there would be no sleep until he had digested his meal. It always amazed him how the Spanish and the Portuguese could eat so late at night and rise so early.

He conjured up a picture of Joseph James Forrester in his mind, took a sip of port and began to write.

If Forrester had had his way port would be a very different drink than it is today. In 1844, at the age of thirty-three, thirteen years after he had joined his uncle's firm, Offley

Forrester, he published an anonymous and intemperate pamphlet that was destined to have the entire port trade in London and Oporto baying for his blood.

In a treatise innocuously entitled 'A Word or Two on Port Wine', Forrester lambasted his fellow shippers for selling what he called 'adulterated wine'. He accused them of encouraging the Douro farmers to add elderberry juice to beef up the colour of their wines. He had questioned the farmers about the practice and guileless as they were they confided to him that they would add as much as twenty-eight pounds of the berries to each pipe. And, on instructions from the shippers, they also poured in sugar or *jeropiga* to sweeten their wines. (Forrester called jeropiga an 'adulterative nectar'. It was, in fact, a form of port — a red wine whose fermentation had been stopped early by the addition of brandy to leave a high residual sugar content in the wine which could be used as a sweetening agent.)

Joe Forrester also railed against the use of brandy in the production of port. He contended that port had always been a 'natural' wine, one which had never seen the addition of brandy during fermentation. The practice of stopping fermentation by the addition of brandy to create a sweet wine had become widespread by the 1840s. Prior to that era — and as early as 1678 — brandy had been added to the finished dry wine merely as a preservative to help it withstand the rigours of the sea voyage to northern European markets. When brandy was used it was only done so sparingly at the final stage before bottling.

Port, as Forrester saw it, was a dry wine, in fact, rather like a cross between claret and Burgundy. But the consumers in nineteenth-century England had gotten used to dark, sweet, powerful wines with high alcohol and the trade was determined to supply them, even if it meant transporting into their Oporto cellars barrels of red Bairrada and Anadian wines to cut with Douro red in order to meet the demand. The addition of brandy weakened the colour and the body of these wines, necessitating the addition of more and more jeropiga.

Forrester had ten thousand copies of his pamphlet printed and its publication hit the Factory House like a bombshell. He had to weather the storm of abuse that followed. Revealed as the anonymous author he was subjected to a barrage of hostility and criticism from his English peers who called him variously a charlatan, a traitor and a turncoat. They dismissed his accusations as 'false and vague' and the motives for his attack were described as 'sinister'.

The Portuguese shippers, on the other hand, stood on the sidelines, delighting in the discomfiture of their English competitors.

Ironically, if Forrester's views had

won the day and the addition of brandy during fermentation had been banned by the Royal Oporto Wine Company (the regulatory body that had controlled the industry since 1756), vintage port would be a dry red wine of up to 14 per cent alcohol rather than the sweet, rich, fruitcake of a fortified wine it is today. It would probably taste like Ferreira's excellent table wine, Barca Velha . . .

Ezra pictured the bluff, ebullient Joseph James Forrester clenching his fists to take on the tightly knit community in which he had to live. His lonely sorties up the valley to chart the river, his photographic and painting expeditions into the Douro hills, suggested a man who had little time for Factory House balls, the formal dinners under cut-glass chandeliers and the English newspapers and magazines that hung from wooden rods on the Reading Room walls.

Not content with papering Oporto with his pamphlets he had taken the fight to England and toured the cities, expounding his philosophy of 'pure wine', untainted by brandy, elderberry juice or sugar. The controversy had raged for several years and the enmity against Forrester grew. His enemies made sure that he was never invited to join the Factory House and some may have thought of going beyond the ultimate social snub. Perhaps there were those whose commercial interests had been so adversely affected by the repercussions of the scandal that they had plotted his death, he speculated. The boatman who took Forrester and his party down the Douro on that fateful Sunday in May could have been bribed by his enemies to lash the rudder the wrong way knowing they would capsize.

Could his dream have been reality? Perhaps there was something in the letters that might give Ezra a clue. But what he could not understand was why Forrester had published the pamphlet in the first place. He must have known that the author of such a contentious document could not remain anonymous for long in such a closed society. Was there a larger issue here? Was it an elaborate smokescreen to cover Forrester's spying activities for the British government? His apparent attack on his own countrymen and his championing of the Douro peasant-growers were the perfect cover for him to trek off into the hills alone with his camera without arousing suspicion. His trip back to England, to carry his message to port's prime market, could also have been a cover for a debriefing by Sir Robert Peel.

Ezra raised his glass in the direction of the river.

'Here's to you, Joe.'

He stood up, stretched and moved to the window. The moon was a wedge of lemon in a sky of black velvet. Through the open window he could hear the wind, the liquid movement of the river and the static sound of crickets. He could barely make out the terraced vines against the granite steps of the darkened hills. The smell of the water mingled with the scent of chestnut and orange trees. The grandfather clock in the hall chimed eleven o'clock.

He was about to undress when he thought he saw a flash of light in the courtyard below. He turned off his bedroom light and moved to the window. He saw a figure moving towards the chapel, guided by the light of a torch. He followed the bouncing light as it illuminated the ornamental fountain and the orange trees behind. He heard the creak of a door opening and then a deep silence.

Ezra, thinking that another incident was in the making, put on his shoes and grabbed his jacket. He opened his bedroom door and felt his way along the darkened corridor to the staircase. The stairs creaked mercilessly under his weight and he was sure that the noise would awaken the household. Careful not to slam the front door, he eased it shut.

The night air was chilly after the heat of the day and the smell of the earth mingled with the scent of French lavender and honeysuckle in his nostrils. The stones under his feet were slick with dew. A gust of wind blew off the river as he edged his way across the courtyard.

The door to the chapel was ajar, emitting a soft orange glow. Slowly he approached it, his heart beginning to thump in his chest.

What if it was the suspected arsonist returned to complete his work?

As his eyes became accustomed to the dark Ezra looked around for something to defend himself with. He saw a pole stuck in a terracotta pot to support a small orange tree. He untwisted the wire that held it to the thin trunk and pulled it from the earth. Holding it across his body with both hands he approached the chapel door.

Peering inside he could see the outline of a veiled figure kneeling in front of a small, painted statue of the Virgin Mary. A lone candle created a halo of light around the supplicant. Her hands were held forward in an attitude of prayer. From the doorway Ezra could see a gold ring on the left hand. He waited for the woman to turn so that he could see her face.

The wind blew again, gusting strongly enough to move the oak door on its creaking hinges. The woman turned towards the sound. Ezra pulled back into the shadows but not before he had caught a glimpse of the long face stained with tears. Embarrassed, he left Helen Sykes to her prayers.

★ ★ ★

Too agitated to sleep, Ezra began to walk down towards the Douro. The velvety black sky above the hills was salted with stars and the moon multiplied its image in each ripple of the river. He could smell the dusty sweetness of the grapes on the vines and the earthy tones of the granite as it gave off its warmth stored up from the heat of the day.

He thought about Helen weeping in front of the Virgin Mary. The ring he touched in his trouser pocket had not been hers. Perhaps it belonged to Amanda Sykes who refused to share her husband's bed. Then there was the unpredictable Luke who bullied his workers and forgot his obligations as a host. The whole quinta seemed to be in a state of turmoil, the Sykes family and their servants included. How could such a dysfunctional household pull off a celebration party, especially when somebody was hell-bent on preventing it from happening at all?

Guided by the light of the moon, Ezra made his way down the rutted track to the road that followed the river bank. It was cooler down here and he could hear the sound of the water agitated by the wind. Behind it was another sound that grew in intensity, that of a car engine.

Ezra looked back in the direction of the sound and saw headlights approaching. He stopped and stood at the side of the road to allow the vehicle to pass. But it slowed down. Caught in its headlights he could not see the car or the driver.

When it came to a stop Ezra recognized it as the white Mercedes he had first seen outside the railway station at Pinhão.

'Mr Ezra Brant, you are walking on the road at night.'

Ezra shielded his eyes from the glare of the lights. It was the voice of Katarina

Soares. He approached the passenger side of the car.

'Good evening, Mrs Soares. I was taking the air. It's a beautiful night.'

Katarina Soares leaned over and opened the door.

'Get in.'

It was more of a command than an invitation. Ezra, slightly irritated but curious, lowered himself into the seat next to her. She was wearing a silk scarf tied tightly around her head and knotted at the throat, white denim pants and a heavy-knit wool sweater.

'Where are we going?' he asked, as the car accelerated along the bumpy road.

'An education, Mr Brant. As a journalist you might be interested.'

Ezra anchored himself to the seat by gripping the door handle. Katarina drove at speed along the narrow, twisting road. The rush of air through the open car made Ezra's eyes water. He recalled the few words he had exchanged with the woman next to him. 'I'm a writer, not a photographer,' he had said, and yet she now called him a 'journalist'. Perhaps she had been doing some investigation of her own.

'Do you mind slowing down. I don't want to end up in the Douro.'

Katarina laughed.

'You don't like speed, Mr Brant? I love speed. Time is precious.'

'My life is precious,' retorted Ezra.

'You have a family?'

'I have a son, Michael, he'll be eighteen in December. I'd really like to get back to celebrate with him.'

She pulled off onto a smaller road that climbed diagonally across the face of sloping vineyard.

'You certainly know your way round here,' said Ezra, who had not even seen the turning although his eyes had been glued to the windscreen.

'This is one of my husband's vineyards. It's not far now.'

The car plunged uphill, its headlights chopping through the inky darkness. As they rounded the hill the road curved into the side of a valley, hidden from the river. Below, at the base of the hill, obscured by a large outcrop of granite, Ezra could see

102

what appeared to be a derelict farmhouse. It was surrounded by old pick-up trucks and jeeps. He could hear a low roar come from inside the abandoned house, followed by whistles and shouts.

Katarina drew the Mercedes up close to a battered old Ford and stepped out. She reached into the pocket of her slacks and took out a packet of cigarettes. She offered him one which he refused and handed him her lighter. Illuminated by its flame her skin looked translucent. He could smell whisky on her breath.

'Keep these in your pocket for me,' she said, handing him the cigarettes and the lighter. 'Come. You have nothing to fear. I know these people.'

Ezra followed her to a set of worn stone steps that led up to a verandah. The noise grew louder. A pale orange light emanated from the grimy windows set in the whitewashed walls.

Katarina Soares pulled open the door. What struck Ezra first was the smell.

Sweat, dust, smoke and blood. By the light of kerosene lamps hooked onto wooden beams, he could see a crush of men leaning into a small lagar. Taller than the rest he was able to peer over the heads of the men and what he saw turned his stomach.

Fighting cocks with metal spurs secured to their legs by leather thongs were doing their best to peck each other's eyes out. Feathers were flying, blood was spurting, a tide of dust rolled across the floor. The stale air was alive with a flurry of anguished squawks and the hoarse imprecations of the spectators waving fistfuls of greasy banknotes as they cheered on their bird.

In one corner stood Vasco leaping from one foot to the other, sweating with excitement. He shook his clenched hands at the combatants, gold tooth shining in the lamplight, urging his cock in for the kill.

So that's how the 'chicken' in the back of the Mercedes had met its fate, thought Ezra.

One bird was down. The stronger of the two now stood on its neck and was savaging its exposed underbelly with its sharp beak. The men roared.

Ezra looked across at Katarina who was standing on a low bench, arms folded across her stomach, swaying her shoulders slightly from side to side as if she were rocking a baby. He caught her eye and his look of repugnance must have registered because she called to him above the din.

'That's life in the Douro,' she said and shrugged.

Vasco picked up his victorious bird and held it high above his head as he strutted around the lagar. He was followed by a boy, probably his son, who collected the money that was held out to him.

The owner of the defeated bird knelt down over the bloody mass of feathers. From the leather sheath on his belt he withdrew a curved pruning knife and dispatched the wounded cock with one slice across its throat. He picked up the dripping carcass, carried it to the edge of the lagar and dropped it unceremoniously into a plastic shopping bag.

The crowd parted to make room for two new contestants who carried their birds into the lagar, holding them out in both hands so that they could see each other. Ezra recognized one of the men. It was Albino Sousa, the Sykes' vineyard manager. He held a hessian sack which contained his own fighting cock.

The two men stood two feet apart in the centre of the lagar pushing the cocks forward at each other to enrage them. Their owners hissed at each other and the men pressing against the granite walls of the lagar hooted and laughed.

The two belligerents eyed each other, their combs erect and livid, their claws raised and tense. Ezra felt his stomach turn. He headed for the door and called to Katarina as he left.

'I'll wait for you outside.'

The woman nodded. The suggestion of a smile played at the corner of her lips.

Ezra was happy to be out in the cold night air. He wandered down through the parked cars to the granite outcrop and sat down. Beads of perspiration dappled his forehead and he felt nauseous. How could she elect to watch such a spectacle, he thought? Was she so bored that only the sight of violent death could awaken her jaded sensitivities? He had to wait for her; there was no way he could find his way back in the dark.

The moon had disappeared behind a cloud and the humid night air began to close in on him like a sweaty palm. The choice of such a remote spot must have meant that cockfighting was illegal in Portugal and the participants had to arrange such competitions by stealth. Katarina's presence did not appear to have upset the men which suggested that she was a frequent spectator at such events. Ezra wondered if her husband accompanied her to them or if he was ignorant of her nocturnal drives through the valley.

In the distance he could hear a siren coming from the direction of Pinhão. Faint at first but definitely coming in his direction. From the rhythm it sounded more like a police car than an ambulance or a fire engine. If it was the police then they were probably coming here, he thought. Someone must have tipped them off.

He hurried back inside the farmhouse to Katarina and whispered in her eat.

'I think the police are coming.'

She nodded and then cupped her hands around her mouth to amplify the sound.

'*Polícia!*' she shouted and immediately the whole room was galvanized into action as if each man knew his allotted task. Birds were scooped up and hustled into bags. Kerosene lamps were unhooked from beams. Feathers were swept up with brooms made from ilex twigs. Buckets of water were splashed over the blood in the lagar. The spectators hurried through the door to their cars and trucks.

'Come with me,' said Katarina, taking Ezra by the hand and leading him quickly to her Mercedes.

The sound of the siren was louder now, bouncing off the hills in an echoing parody of itself. Engines coughed to life, headlights glowed and the vehicles moved off in various directions. Ezra caught sight of Albino Sousa scuttling towards a bicycle, the hessian sack bouncing on his shoulder.

Katarina leaned forward over the steering wheel, roaring with laughter as if she were riding a roller-coaster.

'Why are they using their siren?' asked Ezra.

'That's the whole point. They want us to know they're coming. It happens every time. Cockfighting is forbidden, but here in the Douro there is nothing much to do except watch American television shows. The police know what goes on but they do not want to arrest their cousins and their brothers. Besides, they hate doing paperwork. So they wake up the whole valley with their siren and drive very slowly.'

Ezra sat back in his seat. It made sense. He remembered in the west of Ireland he had visited a pub at the end of a long spit. The pub was notorious in the area for staying open hours after closing time. The owner could see a good five miles across the bay. If the Garda drove out he would simply turn off the lights and lock the front door. The police could have driven without lights, but they never did.

'How do you know Matthew Sykes?' asked Katarina.

'I met him a few times in London. I'm writing a book about port. He's letting me stay at his quinta while I polish off the research.'

Ezra decided that she probably knew that already if she had ears in Quinta do Santo Pedro. He made it sound as if his association with Matthew Sykes was more casual than a friendship.

'Then I hope you will mention us in your book,' said Katarina.

'Perhaps I could visit you. I'd like to take some photographs.'

'We have a photographer visiting us,' Katarina volunteered. 'He's doing a story for the *National Geographic*.'

'I'd like to meet him. I'll need photos for my book.'

'Then you must come and see us. When my husband gets back.'

'When will that be?'

'He may be back already. You never know with Alvaro.'

Katarina slowed down. In the headlights they could see a police car ahead, pulled into the side of the road. Next to it was a truck with no lights. Two officers were leaning against the side panels, questioning the driver.

'That's another of their tricks,' said Katarina. 'They delay their arrival at the cockfight by stopping the first car they see.'

Ezra was thinking about visiting the quinta on the hill above Santo Pedro. Perhaps he had been precipitate in asking Katarina if he could come to see her husband's operation. Was he being disloyal to Matthew Sykes? But it was Matthew who had asked him to sniff around to find out who was determined to ruin their bicentennial celebrations. And besides, he did need some professional photographs and he had not visited many Portuguese houses.

'I don't know how to say this,' began Ezra, 'but I don't want to offend my host. So I'd really like to know what's going on?'

'You mean between Matthew Sykes and my husband?'

'From what I gather there seems to be

111

a certain amount of tension.'

Katarina laughed.

'What is that poem by your poet, Robert Frost? Good fences make good neighbours.'

'Not my poet, but I get your drift. Frost was from New England. I'm Canadian.'

'Of course, how silly of me.'

'You mean you don't have good fences.'

'There is a dispute over land, Mr Brant, a minor matter but it seems to be dragging on forever in the courts. My husband likes to win. I imagine accommodations will be made.'

'What are they disputing?'

'That you will have to ask Mr Sykes or my husband. My role is merely decorative.'

'You sound bitter.'

'I'm a realist. I knew what I was getting into when I married Alvaro. He is a powerful man. And very rich.'

She glanced away out into the darkness of the river and Ezra put a steadying hand on the dashboard. She was silent for a moment and then said:

'Do you believe in reincarnation?'

'No.'

'My husband does. He is convinced in a former life he was Catherine the Great.'

'Really. And that's doesn't bother him?'

'What do you mean?'

'Well, Portuguese men being macho and all that, I'd have thought he'd rather have been Genghis Khan.'

She smiled into the rearview mirror.

'It is not something he jokes about, Mr Brant.'

'And who were you in a previous life, Mrs Soares?'

'Katarina. You must call me Katarina. I — I don't think about these things. If you have no future you have no past.'

'Do you have children?'

'No. Alvaro already has children by his first wife. We all make compromises. What compromises have you made, Mr Brant?'

Compromises. Ezra looked at the side window. He had stayed too many years in a loveless marriage for the sake of Michael only to realize there was no good time in a child's life for him to handle divorce. He had stayed too long as a radio producer with the CBC, fuming at the bureaucracy that stood in the way of creative programme-making yet fearful of giving up the comforts of a staff job for the nakedness of the freelance life. It took courage to change, to break away from familiar patterns and make the leap into the void. There are no compromises once you are committed to the dive.

'I'm going to let you out here,' said Katarina, pulling up at a small side road. 'You can see the quinta from here.'

She pointed to a shadowy mass halfway up the hill.

In front of him, high on the slope, Ezra could see the outline of Quinta do Santo Pedro. On a lower escarpment to his right there was a whitewashed cabin with a tiled roof he had not noticed before. A jeep was parked under a lean-to attached to the wall, presumably to shade the vehicle from the sun. Ezra noticed a faint orange glow coming from one of the windows.

He lingered with his hands resting on the door, reluctant to leave. He was attracted to the woman for her beauty and the aura of sadness that radiated from her like a seductive perfume. He wanted to lift her face to his and kiss her eyes, her lips, and discover her ears under the silken folds of her headscarf. He stretched out his hand and ran the back of his fingers down her cheek.

'Don't,' she said, staring straight in front of her.

'I'm sorry. It's just that you seem so unhappy.'

She turned to him and he could see tears glistening in the corners of her eyes.

Her hands went up to the knot at her throat and began to untie it. Slowly she unwrapped the scarf from her neck and pulled it from her head.

Katarina was completely bald.

'Chemotherapy,' she said. 'The doctors say I am dying of cancer.'

★   ★   ★

The clock struck two as Ezra closed the door of his bedroom. There was no light in the house and no evidence that Luke had returned. He turned on the bedside light and hung up his jacket. He heard the

115

telephone ring in another part of the house and then it stopped.

He was thinking about Katarina and the way they had parted. She had waited to see the expression in his eyes when she revealed her baldness and then she leaned into him and kissed him on the lips. He could still taste her lipstick. He had tried to hold her but she pushed him away and asked him to get out of the car. She accelerated away without a word.

Now he understood her fascination with cockfights and her love of speed. It wasn't boredom; it was the recklessness that comes with the knowledge of death. They say life passes before the eyes of those who drown. He wondered what images flashed through the mind of Joseph Forrester fighting his losing battle against the current at the Cachão de Valeira.

He emptied his pockets and discovered that he still had Katarina's lighter and cigarettes. He held the lighter to his nose and sniffed. Aromas of carbon, petrol and perfume filled his nose. He sighed deeply, placed the lighter on top of the cigarette packet and leaned back on the bed.

Under his left palm he felt something moving beneath the bedclothes. He stood up in alarm and stared at the slight bump in the blanket. Very gingerly, he lifted the bed cover and slowly pulled up the sheet. Exposed to the light a snake coiled itself up into a defensive posture. It was greyish-red in colour with a darker zig-zag down its back defined by black lines. At the end of its snout was a small horn.

Ezra threw the covers down, trembling. He hated snakes. He had no fear of anything that moved on legs, even people. But snakes were his one phobia. He backed to the wall wondering what he should do. He could not awaken the household and let one of the serving girls deal with it. He had to get rid of the thing himself.

He approached the bed with shaking hands and began to untuck the bottom sheet. Drawing all four corners together, including the blankets, he carried the bag-like bundle to the open window and, eyes squeezed tightly shut, he threw it out into the courtyard.

Shaking, he sat down on the edge of the mattress.

Latastes viper, he said to himself. He had come across the horned snake before, the last time he visited Portugal. In a Bairrada vineyard he had nearly stepped on one, curled up in the sun, sleeping at the foot of a vine. The owner of the property pulled him back, laughing. 'It's poisonous,' he had said. 'We get them throughout the Peninsula. Lataste's viper, they're Portugal's only poisonous snake, you know. The rest you find in the Parliament building in Lisbon.'

But how did Portugal's only poisonous snake find its way into his bed? It could not have crawled up and hidden under the bedclothes by itself. It had to have been put there. But who was most likely to know how to handle a venomous snake? Someone who had to be wary of them on a daily basis. Someone who worked in the vineyards.

He turned on all the lights and looked carefully under the bed to see if the snake had a companion. He even checked his suitcase and all the closets, including the small cupboard that acted as a bedside table.

Enervated and unable to sleep Ezra took out the Forrester letters and began to read. Most of them had to do with matters relating to the production of port and domestic inconveniences. Forrester had reiterated his theories to Dona Antonia on how port should be made and bemoaned the jeering reception of his ideas by his fellow shippers. He spoke of plans to refurbish his house in Vila Nova de Gaia, of his groom being kicked by a favourite horse and his housekeeper's rheumatism. But there was one letter to Dona Antonia that caught his attention. It was dated April 20th, 1861, three weeks before Forrester had drowned in the Douro.

I offer you my deep respects, dear lady, and trust that you are continuing to enjoy good health. I have recently returned from England where I gave a paper on vine disease to the Royal Society which, to my gratification, was well received and will be published in their journal (December issue). I shall, of course, forward a copy to you post haste on its arrival. Again I must thank you for your assistance in my research without which I would not have been able to accomplish the task in so short a time.

And now I must trade once more upon our friendship and ask your advice in another matter of a delicate and troubling nature. There is an English family living in Pinhão. The father is Jeremy Livingston Perkins. He is a surveyor, working under contract for a local mining company. His wife Alice Perkins, to fill the hours when her husband is not at home, had started a class to teach the local children English at no expense to them or their families. In the course of this instruction she has been reading from the King James Bible. It would appear that this has caused some acrimony among the local inhabitants who are fearful that she is attempting to proselytise their children in her own religion. There may or may not be a causal connection between the two circumstances but her seven-year-old son, an only child whose name is Jonathan, has been kidnapped and a ransom in gold demanded. Mr Perkins immediately contacted the local constabulary as well as the British Consul to Lisbon. But the boy has not been found and there is no clue as to where he might be hidden. Fearing for the child's safety, his father had determined that he will pay the ransom as demanded but has not been able to raise the required amount.

Mr Perkins made the journey to my offices in Oporto to enlist my help in the matter this very morning. I was moved to tears by his story and the plight of his young son and will do what I can to help, if only to provide the necessary funds so that the ransom can be raised. You will recall that the kidnapping of small children of the Anglican faith is not unknown in Portugal. From the mid-1600s until well into the new century Protestant children were abducted from their homes on instructions from the Inquisition and secreted in monasteries where they were instructed in the Catholic faith. Since a ransom has been demanded there is little doubt that the motives in this case are pecuniary rather than perceived religious salvation. This is the judgement of our mutual friend, the Bishop of Oporto D. Jerónimo Rebello (whose portrait I painted ten years ago you may recall).

My request to you as a mother and my friend is that you ask your farmers at your property, Quinta do Porto, to make enquiries as to the whereabouts of a fair-haired boy of seven years, with blue eyes, who may be held in some remote farmhouse. Time, you will agree, is of the essence. May I counsel discretion in this matter and I look forward to hearing from you at your earliest convenience.

I remain, your devoted friend, J. J. Forrester.'

Ezra put the letter down and began thinking about the Perkins. Every parent's nightmare — a child snatched from home. How frantic they must have been, strangers in a remote community, trying to adapt and fit in. And here was Joseph Forrester, separated from his own children with a Victorian attitude towards them, willing to become involved to alleviate another man's grief.

A mosquito whined in his ear with the persistence of a dentist's drill. He turned on the light and stalked it around the room until it settled on a wall. With the flat of his palm he squashed it and when he withdrew his hand there was a mark of blood on the wall. He wondered if it was his.

He fell asleep in his clothes that night, thinking of his own son whom he might never have seen again if he had slid mindlessly between the sheets.

★ ★ ★

Ezra was awoken the next morning by the sound of laughter beneath his window. Groggy, he eased himself upright, momentarily surprised to find himself completely dressed. He crossed to the window and looked through the shutter. Gertrudes and her daughter Anna were folding up his bed linen.

Ezra threw open the shutters and bellowed at them.

'Snake! Be careful of the snake.'

Shielding their eyes from the sun the two women looked up at him and then at each other. They shrugged in unison and continued to fold the sheets that flashed blindingly white in the morning light.

He was about to try to explain when there was a knock at the bedroom door.

'Come in.'

Helen Sykes stood in the doorway holding a small tray with a tea cup, a teapot, a bowl of sugar and a small jug of milk.

'Good morning,' she said.

There were violet rings under her eyes.

'Good morning.'

'Was the room too hot for you last night?'

'No, no. It was fine,' he said, taking the tray from her. 'It was just that there was something moving in the bed and I'm afraid I panicked. I warned the cook and the maid but they just laughed at me.'

'Ah,' said Helen. 'Yes, we do get spiders . . . What will you have for breakfast? Eggs and bacon?'

'Just toast, thank you. And coffee.'

She was about to leave and Ezra spoke again.

'Tell me, Helen. That little house in the vineyard. Is it a guest cottage?'

'I'm not sure I know what you mean.'

'You can just see it from here.'

Helen approached the window and looked out in the direction of his pointing finger.

'Oh that. Sometimes we put up our guests there if there's no room in the main house.'

'Does Luke sleep there?'

Helen reddened. Ezra watched the blood rising in her neck and blooming hotly in her cheeks.

'Why do you ask?'

'I thought I saw his jeep parked there last night.'

'Everybody drives jeeps here,' said Helen and there was an anger in her tone that took Ezra aback.

She turned and left the room without a further word.

* * *

Luke was not present at breakfast. There was a copy of yesterday's London *Times* on the table next to his place setting. A snowy white napkin in a silver ring, a pot of coffee, a jar of marmalade set on a silver saucer, a pat of deep yellow butter melting in the heat and a toast rack with four pieces of white toast standing upright, their crusts cut off.

Ezra could never understand the function of toast racks. He had been given a silver one by an English friend as a wedding present which he now used to file unanswered correspondence.

When Anna came to clear away his breakfast things he announced that he was going for a walk and that if anyone was looking for him he would be in the vineyard.

Negotiating the route down to the guest cottage was rather like descending the pyramids of Gizah. The terraces allowed for three rows of vines and then fell steeply away. They were buttressed by ancient walls made of the rocks that had been gouged out of the earth two centuries ago with hand spikes and shovels. The vines on their wire trellises, heavy with fruit, were supported by stakes of locally quarried slaty schist, standing like solemn totems.

Ezra was sweating when he arrived at the small house. Standing in the shade of an olive tree he mopped his brow with a handkerchief and cursed himself for not wearing a hat. The jeep was no longer in the lean-to. He tried the front door and it opened easily. Stepping inside he found himself in a large room in the centre of which was an old-fashioned pot-bellied stove and a stack of dried vine trunks. In one corner stood an ornately carved Victorian bedstead next to which was a small fridge that acted as a bedside table. He opened it. Inside was a bottle of mineral water and beside it a bottle of port. He took it out. It was a ten-year-old tawny, an inch or two left, and it bore a Quinta do Coterio label. The glass was sticky to the touch and there were stains on the label where the wine had dribbled down the bottle.

On the other side of the room by the largest window was a circular wooden table and three chairs. In the centre stood a long black torch. He picked it up and switched it on. It gave out an orange beam of light; the batteries were low.

A door to the right led to a tiny bathroom that was fitted with a shower. The towel that hung from the rod on the wall was damp. A bar of Imperial Leather soap, the kind his father used to use, was sitting in a plastic dish on the washbasin. There were dried bubbles on its surface. A bottle of Dettol and a crepe bandage stood on a glass shelf inside a cabinet set over the basin.

Ezra returned to the main room and crossed to the bed. The blankets were tucked in army-style. He lifted the pillow and sniffed it. There was a faint smell of a woman's fragrance or maybe a man's after-shave. Or maybe both.

Ezra's search of the room was interrupted by the sound of trucks on the road below. He went outside in time to see a fleet of three vehicles turning off the main road onto the property. Their trailers were laden with men and equipment. They were led up the drive by Luke in his jeep, almost obliterated from view by the red dust kicked up by their massive wheels.

When he reached the farmhouse the trucks and Luke were nowhere to be seen. But Matthew Sykes was sitting in the living room reading the newspaper. He rose to greet Ezra.

'My dear fellow, they been looking after you all right, have they?'

Ezra marvelled at the fact that Sykes was wearing his habitual three-piece suit. The only concession to the heat was the removal of the gold watch chain.

'Very well, thank you. What were all those trucks?'

'The marquee. I rented it from the

Factory House. Very decent price. Got to protect my guests from the heat. They're erecting it in the new vineyard. Now that it's been levelled it's more accessible. Chairs and tables, that sort of thing, barbecues. But tell me, have they made you comfortable, Helen, Gertrudes and the rest?'

'I've been very well looked after. Food's terrific.'

'Yes, Gertrudes is a gem, isn't she. Been with the family for years. Loyalty. Put a lot of store by that. Now tell me what do you want to do?'

'Well, would you like me to bring you up to date on what's been happening?'

'Later, later, dear boy. Perhaps you'd like to see the treading.'

'I saw that last night. I even got into the lagar.'

'Splendid, splendid. Perhaps you'd like to go out on the water.'

'Did Luke tell you about the fire?'

'Yes, yes. It's all under control though. How's the book coming?'

'Fine,' said Ezra, puzzled by Sykes' effervescent mood. He was about to bring up the matter of the snake and the bedclothes but he decided to wait. From his experience of country house weekends in England he knew that every occurrence that was slightly deviant from the norm was a subject for exhaustive analysis and comment. The servants would gossip to Helen and she might have told Sykes of his strange behaviour. Ezra had expected a jocular 'Hot in the night were you, old boy?' but Sykes had made no reference to the incident. Instead, he asked:

'The letters interesting, are they?'

'The letters are great. I haven't had a chance to read them all but they are helping me shape a theory.'

'You must tell me all about it,' said Sykes, placing an arm around Ezra's shoulders and leading him towards the door.

'Now I feel I've abandoned you too long. How can I make it up to you?'

'I'd really like to see where the Forrester letters were found.'

'In the dovecot, I told you.'

'Will you take me there?'

'If you really want to see it, of course.

Anything you like, old boy.'

'And at some point I'd like to see where he actually drowned.'

Sykes patted him on the back.

'A bit morbid this morning, aren't we?'

Sykes reached for a large straw hat from the stand in the hall and handed it to Ezra.

'You'll need this.'

He chose a Panama for himself and withdrew a sturdy cane from the elephant's foot bin.

They walked out into glaring sunlight. The jeep had been parked in the shade of the wall outside the courtyard. Ezra put on his sunglasses and Sykes slipped out of his jacket and folded it neatly on the back seat of the jeep, headless of the dust that had accumulated on the hot leather. He seemed preoccupied as if he was going through the motions of being a good host but would rather be elsewhere.

'I'm afraid I haven't got much to report,' said Ezra. 'You heard about the fire.'

'Yes. Don't think it's got anything to do with the business we talked about though.

One of those freak accidents. But everything's under control.'

He lapsed into silence again, concentrating on the bumpy track between the vineyards.

'I managed to have a brief conversation with your son,' said Ezra. 'He certainly has some strong opinions on the future direction of your company.'

Sykes said nothing.

'I'm sure he's told you he wants you to build a cellar up here so you can age your ports here rather than in Gaia.'

Sykes nodded, staring directly ahead through the dusty windscreen.

'And he wants to make a red wine that will rival a first-growth Bordeaux.'

'Did he give you a barrel sample?'

'No, he never mentioned he'd actually made one.'

'He has a couple of French barrels hidden away at the back of the cellar. He thinks I don't know about them. Children, Ezra, they think their fathers are fools.'

Sykes turned off the track to a rutted path just wide enough to allow the jeep through. Canes from the vines whipped the sides of the vehicle as they drove by. They were climbing again and could no longer see the quinta buildings. Below him, Ezra watched a line of women in blue skirts moving between the vines harvesting the grapes. Their menfolk carried the full baskets on their shoulders to a waiting flatbed truck.

'That's the dovecot up there,' said Sykes, bringing the jeep to a stop. It was a circular building with whitewashed walls, about four metres in diameter, with a flat-tiled roof that rose to a point in the centre. Three doves were perched on the tiles.

'May I see inside?' asked Ezra.

'It's not used now,' said Sykes. 'It's pretty dirty. Bird droppings, you know.'

'Still, I'd be interested.'

Ezra was out of the jeep before the older man could protest. He had to step over a low wall and follow it up the terraces to where the dovecot was positioned in the middle of the vineyard.

The vines, Ezra noticed, were straggly and unkempt. He worked his way along the rows, looking back to see if Sykes was following. He stood in shade of the whitewashed walls as he waited. Sykes had put on his jacket and was moving cautiously over the broken ground as if it were a minefield.

The inside of the dovecot was cool and damp. It smelled of wet granite, ammonia and rotting leaves. Ezra had expected to find a network of pigeonholes filled with cooing doves but instead there were merely wooden rafters streaked with bird droppings and no doves. Then he recalled Sykes telling him about Vasco finding doves poisoned on the roof.

'Where did Vasco come across the letters?'

Sykes led him to the curved part of the wall that was built into the side of the slope. There was a crossbeam that supported the structure from which a smaller beam angled up to carry the weight of the roof. Sykes pointed to the cleft where they met.

'The bundle was wedged in there.'

'How do you think they came to be here?' asked Ezra.

'This property used to belong to Dona Antonia Ferreira, as did virtually all the land on this side of the Douro.'

'But why would she have hidden them here?'

Perhaps there were love letters among them, was the thought uppermost in his mind.

'There's probably some innocent explanation, old boy. A robbery maybe, a remorseful thief who couldn't bring himself to destroy the — '

The sound of a rifle shot ricocheting off the impacted mud wall of the dovecot made Sykes stop in mid-sentence.

'Get down,' he whispered.

Bewildered, Ezra slid down the wall next to Sykes who was already crouching.

'What's going on?'

Sykes reached into the inside pocket of his jacket and took out his cellphone. Angrily, he punched in the numbers.

'Luke,' he said, and then he began speaking rapidly in Portuguese. At the end of the conversation he put the phone back in its holster and pursued his lips. Ezra realized that his host had lapsed into

Portuguese so that he would not under-stand the conversation and he felt angry at being excluded.

'Matthew, what the hell's going on?'

'Nothing serious, old boy, just a local turf war. This vineyard technically belongs to Quinta do Coteiro.'

'What the hell are you talking about? We were shot at.'

'Yes, it was a warning only. They weren't aiming at us.'

'They were still shooting at us. And last night I found a goddamned viper in my bed.'

'A viper in your bed . . . So that explains the blanket episode.'

Sykes was laughing.

'I don't see what's so funny. You asked me to come here and find out who's trying to sabotage your birthday party. And now I'm involved. I could have been bitten by a poisonous snake and it's all a big joke.'

'I'm sorry. I owe you an explanation, Ezra. I just phoned Luke and he's going to make sure we get out of here safely. He'll call us when the coast is clear.'

137

'But what the hell's going on?'

'This vineyard is in dispute between me and my neighbour Mr Soares up there at the top of the hill. It's one small part of an ongoing legal battle. The Soares family used to own both properties up until the French Revolution. One of Soares' ancestors was a great friend of Marie Antoinette and was visiting her in Paris when she was taken by the mob. He was in her party trying to escape Versailles. And he was thrown in prison. The Jacobins believed he was a spy for the king of Portugal. He was all set to follow Louis XVI to the guillotine when his family interceded with Mirabeau who demanded a huge ransom for his safe passage back to Lisbon. To raise the money the family had to sell off the part of the property that is now Quinta do Santo Pedro. That's when my family bought it. Dona Antonio Ferreira purchased the upper part, Coteiro, from my great-great-grandfather, John Sykes. On her death the Soares family bought it from her. Now Alvaro Soares wants the whole estate back and is suing me for it.'

'But if you have the notarized deed of sale what's the problem?'

'It's not that simple. John Sykes was the first Sykes to ship port and he bought the property from a bank that loaned the Soares family the ransom money. They were holding the title deeds as collateral. The principal was to be paid back within forty years otherwise they forfeited the vineyards. As luck would have it, the end of the term came smack dab in the middle of the Civil War of the Two Brothers, Dom Pedro, the former emperor of Brazil, and his brother Miguel. Dom Pedro eventually prevailed but not before the Miguelites had laid siege to Oporto. The last thing they did before retreating was to dynamite the Wine Company's lodge in Vila Nova de Gaia. The streets ran purple with 27,000 pipes of port, much of it from the Soares family properties. It took them twenty-five years to recover financially but they lost the property to the bank. Alvaro Soares has made a fortune in copper in Chile and now his dream is to reunite the family vineyards.

Over my dead body, I might add.'

'Then it's Soares who is trying to undermine your celebration.'

'That was my first thought, obviously. But the incidents could only have been perpetrated by someone on my own estate.'

'Tell me, Matthew, if you had been Portuguese, your family that is, rather than English, would the same thing be happening?'

Sykes was sitting on the hard earth floor, his pale, tapering hands resting at the wrist on his knees. He coughed and stared at the ceiling for a moment before replying.

'To understand the relationships in the Douro you need to know a little of the history. Forgive me if I sound like a schoolmaster for a moment but you'll see where I'm leading. Port, as you know, has always had a special place on the Englishman's table and that predilection has as much to do with *Realpolitik* as it does with any sensory delight. In 1703 the British negotiated a treaty with the Portuguese, part of our Grand Alliance against the French. The Methuen Treaty, as it was known, had commercial implications too. Cloth made from English wool could be exported to Portugal free of duty while Portuguese wine could be imported into Britain at a third of the tariff placed on French wines. So, naturally, the trade in port and Madeira flourished. Of course the Scots, being Scots and natural allies of the French against the English, insisted on drinking claret. The more claret they drank the more port we drank, a sort of bibulous patriotism, I suppose. Well, as you can imagine, the demand for port soon outstripped its supply which led to some unscrupulous practices, such as the addition of sweet Spanish wines, elderberries and even the blood of young bulls. But then you know all about that from your researches.

'In the mid-eighteenth century the market began to fall apart because the English refused to drink such terrible wines. So the shippers read the riot act to the growers — if they didn't stop adulterating their wines we would refuse to buy them. Well, of course, this caused a real donnybrook between the English shippers, represented by the Factory, and the Portuguese farmers. The growers brought their case to their Prime Minister, the Marquis of Pombal, who took the position that the English shippers had insulted the integrity of the Portuguese. He immediately turned the entire industry into a state monopoly. To do this he set up the Companhia Geral da Agrigultura dos Vinhos do Alto Douro which would fix the price of wine for export. You can imagine this was one in the eye for the English shippers. The Old Wine Company, as it was known, told the shippers how much they could export and the price they had to pay for the wines. Pombal also delimited the area where port wine could be grown. This was completed in 1771, which makes port the first wine to have its own appellation of origin. You'll see those granite markers on the properties that demarcate the area from which port for export can be grown. There's one over at the corner of this vineyard. You may have seen a granite post that looks like a gravestone. It has the word 'Feitoria' carved on it with the date or a number. Feitoria means factory.'

'Didn't they also classify the vineyards then?' asked Ezra.

'Yes. Each property listed within the demarcated area was accorded a price for its wine, so many *reis* per pipe, and their production was estimated based on an average of the previous five vintages. The growers could not sell more pipes than the figure in the index. At this time the best vineyards were owned by the Jesuits. Like this one. In fact, all the land you can see on the other side of the Douro was owned by the See of the Archbishop of Braga. There has always been an uneasy truce between the British and the Portuguese shippers. I suppose it's only human nature that they would want all their soil to be owned by native sons. But we do things in different ways. It would be very boring if we all did it the same, what?'

The cellphone at his hip rang and he pulled it out and pressed the receive button.

'Hello . . . Fine . . . Thank you.'

Sykes put the phone away again.

'We can go now. There won't be any trouble.'

'Does this happen all the time? If you wander onto his property?' asked Ezra, as they emerged into the sunlight.

'You mean taking potshots? Oh, he'd deny it of course. Say it was a stray bullet from a hunter's gun. But I know.'

Ezra looked for the mark on the wall. There was a chunk of plaster missing from the wall just below the tiles, exposing a patch of dried mud and straw the size of a hand below the whitewashed surface. The shot, he reasoned, must have come from above. He looked up the vineyard into the sun. He saw someone, a man, standing on a wall. Instinctively, he ducked behind the dovecot.

'There's someone up there,' he whispered to Sykes, who was busy checking a bunch of grapes for ripeness.

'It's all right. Luke has phoned them to call off the dogs. Can't have a journalist caught in the crossfire can we?'

Ezra had been shot at once before. Two

years ago in Barbaresco, in a restaurant with a beautiful Irish woman. The shot had hit a bottle of wine above his head and he was drenched in wine. Which, in retrospect, was better than being drenched in blood. Anger warred with apprehension as he peeked around the side of the dovecot. The man had a tripod suitable for holding a rifle with a telescopic sight. But instead of a rifle it was mounted with a camera and a long lens.

'He's got a camera.'

'Well, show him your best side and let's get back to the house.'

Sykes spat out a grape skin and returned to the jeep without even looking up at the photographer. Behind him was the dusty van Ezra had first seen at Pinhão railway station.

★ ★ ★

Lunch had been set in the courtyard on a table under the shade of the eucalyptus tree. Helen was waiting for them, placing napkins on each plate. A large dish of cold chicken, ham and hardboiled eggs was already attracting flies. Bowls of salad and fresh fruit and large circular loaves of bread completed the meal. Two bottles of white wine that looked like Vinho Verde were chilling in an ice bucket.

'Luke says you should start without him,' said Helen, addressing herself to Sykes. 'He's receiving the grapes now.'

'Would you like to freshen up?' Sykes asked Ezra.

'Sure. I'll be down in a moment.'

The maid had closed the shutters to keep the sunlight out of the room. It was semi-dark and Ezra moved stealthily, groping for the light switch, fearful of snakes. Something was troubling him about his host's behaviour. He could not formulate what it was but the Englishman seemed to have taken the shooting incident very lightly, as if it were a common occurrence. Either that, or he placed little value on his own life — and by association, mine too, thought Ezra. Nor did he seem interested in learning what I have found out here.

The bed had been made and he tested

its surface gingerly before sitting down. In three days, the guests would be arriving. The house would be full and, no doubt, all the hotel rooms in Pinhão had been reserved. Yet the mysterious incidents continued to happen. He wondered what the real purpose of his presence at Quinta do Santa Pedro was.

Ezra had a feeling that Helen Sykes was the key to the family secrets; Helen and perhaps in some way the Forrester letters. He did not believe for one moment that historical documents as important as these could have been hidden for over one hundred years in a dovecot.

He rose from the bed and opened his suitcase. The letters were in an oilskin pack, a little larger than a tobacco pouch. He sniffed the shiny surface. There was no smell reminiscent of the inside of the dovecot. He put the bundle into the light satchel he carried for his camera and notebook and crossed to the bathroom to douse cold water on his hands and face.

Matthew Sykes and Helen were seated at the table when he returned. From the look on the woman's face Ezra could tell their conversation had upset her. She sat, shoulders hunched, her hands in her lap, eyes downcast. Sykes was smoking a cigarette, something Ezra had never seen him do. He flicked it casually into the bushes as Ezra approached the table.

'A glass of Vinho Verde, old boy. Nothing like it on a hot summer's day. As fresh as lemon juice and lively as champagne. A greatly underestimated wine.'

Sykes splashed the wine into Ezra's glass.

'Just been telling Helen about our little shooting gallery up there. Sounded like a two-two, wouldn't you say? Good for rabbits, that's about it.'

'I don't know how you can joke about it, Matthew,' chided Helen.

Ezra was surprised to hear her use Sykes' first name. He would have thought that English propriety dictated that she call him Uncle Matthew to his face.

'No good going to pieces over it, my dear. Ezra here will have some good colour for his book.'

In the distance he could hear the

rhythmic sound of metal hitting metal. The workmen were probably erecting the marquee in the vineyard, driving the metal guy-line pegs into the stony ground. The echoing sound reminded him of his camping trips with Michael into Northern Ontario lakes. Bonding trips they were meant to be, father and son canoeing and fishing together. But all Michael wanted to do was sleep and it was on one of these trips that Ezra caught him smoking. He was fifteen. But he remembered the trips fondly and Michael treasured the memory more than the actual experience.

Fish had never tasted as good as the walleye they pan-fried over an open fire with potatoes baked in mud in the embers. Everything he needed to know in life, Ezra was convinced, he had learned in the Boy Scouts. The rest was merely manners.

'What is the book you're writing?' asked Helen.

'It's about port but I think it will end up being more about the Baron de Forrester.'

'I read a biography of him. Didn't John Delaforce write one?'

The question was directed at Sykes.

'Dear old John, yes, quite the scholar. Wrote a history of the Factory House too. Bit of a laundry list though.'

'Would you like me to serve you?' asked Helen.

'By all means,' replied Ezra.

She stood up and leaned over the table, her back to the sun. Her arms were red and the sunlight shining through her light cotton dress illuminated the shape of the body it covered. She wore no bra and the weight of her breasts pressed against the fabric. She had a remarkably good figure which she seemed to hide with her poor posture and her retiring manner.

Ezra could see that Sykes too was studying her and from the corner of his eye he became aware that Luke was approaching her from behind. He put his finger to his lips to silence any greeting and tiptoeing up to her he grabbed her by the waist.

'Tadd-ah!'

Helen screamed and threw the serving

spoons in the air and then collapsed into her seat. Luke sprawled into his, laughing uproariously, while his father frowned and looked away up the hill.

'You gave me such a fright.'

Helen's face had turned as red as her arms.

'Sorry, cousin. You know, I can see right through your dress.'

'Luke! Leave the poor girl alone, will you,' snapped Matthew.

Luke raised his arms in mock surrender. Helen sat bolt upright in her chair, her arms wrapped tightly across her chest. Ezra, embarrassed, wondered if he should change the mood by telling the family about his nocturnal exploits at the cockfight. But since he would have to invoke the name of Katarina Soares whose husband had just ordered someone to scare them off the property with a rifle, he decided to opt for a less controversial topic.

'You were asking about my book, Helen. I had a dream about it on the way up here in the train. It was after that marvellous lunch we had at the Factory

House, Matthew. I don't usually sleep on trains but it was hot and I'd probably had too much port. Anyway, I had this dream and it was just so vivid. I was standing on the rocks above the rapids at Valeira — '

'There are no rapids at Valeira,' Luke cut in.

'Let the man speak,' said his father, sternly.

'Yes, I know. That's the whole point. I was looking down at the raging water. It was almost as if I had been there in another life. I saw the wreckage of Joseph Forrester's boat. The sail was in the water. There were women screaming, being carried downriver, their crinolines ballooning out in front of them. And a man hanging on to a barrel for dear life, but it smashed against the rocks and flooded him with olive oil. And there in the middle of it all was Forrester. I could see his face. I knew it was him.'

'How did you know it was Forrester?' Luke interrupted him again.

'I've seen photographs of him. Anyway, he's swimming madly for the shore but the current is too strong. The boatman has already made it to safety and he's standing on the rocks with his long paddle. He extends it out to Forrester who's desperately trying to catch hold of it. The boatman is holding the paddle out as far as he can reach and finally Forrester grabs the end of it. The boatman begins to haul him in but then he changes his grip on the paddle and he drives it into Forrester's chest. The end is lodged in his waistcoat and he's pushed under the water. I'm shouting and trying to get to the water's edge but I'm too high up.'

'What happened then?' demanded Luke.

'I woke up.'

'So you dreamed that Forrester was murdered by his boatman,' said Luke, cocking his head to one side and smiling at Ezra.

'It was just too real,' said Ezra.

'You've been reading too many books or drinking too much port,' laughed Luke.

He looked over at Matthew Sykes who shook his head.

'Impossible,' said the older Sykes. 'His

people were always loyal to him. Forrester drowned because his boots filled with water. And he was wearing a money belt.'

'A money belt?' enquired Ezra.

'Gold coins, to pay his growers. Weighed him down.'

'How do you know that?'

'Haven't you read the accounts?' snapped Sykes, testily.

'But his body was never found.'

'That's right.'

'But where was it recorded that he had gold on him?'

Sykes seemed angered by Ezra's persistence.

'Perhaps it's in the bloody letters. How should I know, man?'

Something was bothering Matthew Sykes. He had never known him to be in such a prickly mood.

'Dreams can be very real,' murmured Helen, more to herself than as her contribution to the conversation.

Ezra saw Luke roll his eyes. Helen sat like a statue, staring at her feet.

Yes, thought Ezra, the answer might well be in the letters. Forrester wore a money belt full of gold pieces three weeks after he had written to Dona Antonia about the kidnapped boy. Supposing Dona Antonia had found out from her workers at Quinta do Porto where Jonathan Perkins had been hidden; and suppose Forrester, who had an intimate knowledge of the country, had taken it on himself to travel to some remote village in the mountains above Sabrosa to negotiate for the boy's release and to pay the kidnappers' ransom demand. Forrester had left the Quinta de Vesúvio with Dona Antonia and her party on a Sunday when the workers would be at home for the day of rest. They were heading west down the Douro en route to Régua, the city at the western limit of port's demarcated region, where Dona Antonia had her villa. If the ill-fated *rabelo* had made it through the cataract, Forrester could have disembarked at Pinhão and continued his journey north by mule.

But if someone had learned the reason for his trip and the fact that he was carrying gold they might have bribed the boatman to lash the rudder the wrong way . . . .

These speculations flashed through Ezra's mind in the silence that followed Helen's remark. Matthew Sykes slumped in his chair, frowning. Luke continued to stare at Helen with a mocking smile on his lips and she sat rigidly staring at the ground. The tableau might have remained like this for some time had Vasco not opened the metal door to the courtyard and insinuated himself inside. He approached Sykes respectfully and whispered in his ear. His employer nodded and rose.

'It seems we have a visit from the local constabulary. Probably about the shooting incident. Now there's no need for you to get involved in this,' he said, addressing himself to Ezra. 'Either you can take the jeep and drive around and see what you want to see or Luke can take you out in the boat.'

'I'm sorry, Dad. Much as I'd like to, but I have to supervise the crush. Perhaps another time.'

'All right,' said Sykes, frostily. 'Then

you can take the jeep, Ezra. The keys are in the glove compartment. So if you'll excuse me I'll just go and put on my jacket.'

'Of course,' said Ezra.

★   ★   ★

When Ezra passed through the gate he saw a police car parked next to the jeep. Two men inside, one in uniform, the other in plain clothes, watched him as he slid into the driver's seat. There is a natural tendency to feel guilty when observed by law enforcement officers so Ezra's movements were deliberately casual. He took his time leaning over to the glove compartment and reaching for the ignition key. Under it was a map which he took out as well. He made a great play of buckling his seatbelt, checking the rearview mirror and adjusting his seat. He did not glance at the men in the car as he backed up to turn around but he could feel their eyes boring into him.

He drove slowly down the track,

looking back until he could no longer see the police car. The pickers were working the lower slopes now and at the end of the rows of vines the woven baskets overflowing with dusty, purple grape bunches were waiting for the tractors to convey them to the lagares. He pulled up at the main road and studied the map. He located Quinta do Santo Pedro and traced the route that would take him up to Alvaro Soares' property. He had two missions there — to return Katarina's lighter and cigarettes and to find out why Soares had ordered his men to shoot at trespassers on sight. Or maybe it was Soares himself who had pulled the trigger.

Ezra looked for a back road up to Quinta do Coteiro as he did not want members of the Sykes' household to know he was visiting their neighbour. Under a blazing sun, he drove up a rocky track, bouncing the jeep from side to side. It took him longer than he thought to reach the summit of the hill but when he did the view was spectacular. The whole valley was laid out before him, a vast carpet of undulating vineyards, like petrified waves, defining the contours of the hills. The vines around grew like tortured black limbs out of the sandy soil, their bright green leaves and fat purple grapes Nature's reward for their troll-like ugliness. The river below reflected the blue of the sky and the cotton-ball clouds that hung suspended over the distant peaks. Strange to think of this place in winter, bitterly cold and grey and everything dead.

The sight of the gleaming stainless steel tanks told him that he had reached Quinta do Coteiro. He passed through a set of tall wrought-iron gates along a wide gravel path, lined with palm trees and cypresses. On both sides were lawns as manicured as putting greens. Sprinklers sent sheets of water arcing over them, creating brilliant little rainbows. The house in front of him was executed in honey-coloured granite. The lower storey was a series of square columns and circular arches that threw the inner façade into deep shadow. The upper storey was a long verandah, heavy with vines and climbing roses. The red-tiled roof sloped up to a central bell tower. Attached to the house was a chapel with a smaller tower mimicking that over the house. Parked to the left of the house was the white Mercedes.

The house exuded an air of permanence and stability as if it had been there forever, commanding the highest hill in the vicinity and dominating its neighbours. As Ezra drove up a man in a white waiter's jacket and black trousers appeared from out of the shadows. Ezra drew up beside him.

'Do you speak English?'

The man nodded.

'I've come to see Mrs Soares.'

'You will wait here, please.'

He disappeared inside and Ezra alighted from the jeep. He took off his hat and wiped the sweat from his brow. From here he could not see the obtrusive stainless steel tanks or the helicopter pad that Luke had told him about.

A moment of panic struck Ezra. What if Katarina was not at home, sleeping or having therapy or too ill to see him? He would have to explain to her husband why he had come to the house. For her own protection and for his, he could hardly tell Alvaro Soares that his wife had picked him up on the road at night and taken him to a cockfight and here he was returning her cigarettes.

He had already determined his strategy: he would go on the offensive, confronting Soares with the shooting incident in the vineyard.

A tall man with jet-black hair wearing a crisply pressed suit the colour of old piano keys, a black shirt and white patent leather shoes emerged from the shadows. He was smoking a fat cigar. On the first knuckle of the baby finger of his right hand he wore the cigar's band like a ring. The sweet smell of the smoke wafted by Ezra's nostrils. Cuban, and very fine.

Ezra estimated his age at fifty-two. His face was that of an El Greco saint, elongated and gaunt with the penetrating black eyes of a zealot. There was a line under the long, bony nose to the thin, bluish lips that suggested surgery to repair a cleft palate. When Soares spoke he had a faint lisp he obviously laboured to overcome, carefully enunciating each word.

'Good afternoon, Mr Brant. My wife told me to expect your visit.'

Ezra breathed an inward sigh of relief. He had mentally made the excuse for his visit that he was looking for the photographer Katarina had picked up at the station.

Alvaro Soares spoke good English and seemed to enjoy the flourish of his language. Ezra could see that he was scrutinizing him as they walked towards the house.

'Thank you. I apologise for arriving unannounced. I had the loan of this jeep so I just thought I'd drive up.'

'The jeep of Mr Matthew Sykes,' remarked Soares, taking Ezra by the elbow and leading him inside.

'Yes, I'm staying at his quinta.'

'I know that.'

Ezra took a calculated gamble.

'Then why did someone on your property shoot at me this morning?'

Soares stopped and turned to face him.

Ezra determined to meet the fixed stare with his own.

'I must apologize,' said Soares, with a sweeping gesture of his hand. 'It is not our habit to fire weapons at journalists who are visiting our country. One of my workers, a new man, straight from his military service, you understand. He saw a rabbit in the vineyard and he thought, 'ahah! Dinner.' Come, I will make it up to you.'

In spite of himself, Ezra felt drawn to the man.

The room he found himself in was large and airy. The wooden furniture was painted in the fashion of the Alentejo region. The white walls were hung with abstract paintings, startling in their vivid colours, contrasting with the heavy wood furniture and the ornately carved stone fireplace that dominated the end wall. On closer inspection Ezra recognized that the intricate figures that seemed to be drowning in the stone depicted Dante's *Inferno*. He had seen something like that on a church door in Spain.

'My wife tells me that you are writing a

book about port. I would very much like you to try our wines so that you can write about Quinta do Coteiro. We are the oldest quinta in the province, although some would dispute this, but it is true. The Soares family have been farming here for thirteen generations. I will give you the documentation. How do you call it? Press kit.'

'Yes. And how is Mrs Soares?'

'Please, sit down.'

He indicated the white sofa with its cushions covered in a glitzy fabric Ezra had only seen in Morocco. Tiny circular mirrors the size of the smallest coins were sewn into the design.

'My wife is resting. She finds the heat very tiring. May I offer you a drink? A whisky perhaps. You must be bored by port now. We do tend to present it always to our guests like a newborn baby. How about a Bourbon?'

'Do you have any rye?'

'Rye. Yes. You are Canadian. I'm sorry. I have no rye but I have a selection of single malts you may find interesting. Come, you can choose for yourself.'

He crossed to a wooden wall cabinet painted with flowers and opened it. Immediately the inner light went on, illuminating four long shelves stocked with bottles. There must have been eighty different malts there. Ezra ran his eye over the labels and noticed that each shelf held the products of a specific region: Lowlands on the bottom, above it the Highlands, then Campbeltown and, on the top, Islay. He chose a Highland Park from the Orkneys, Scotland's most northerly single malt distillery.

'I will take Glenmorangie,' said Soares, reaching for two crystal glasses. Using silver tongs, he lifted ice cubes from a silver ice bucket and dropped them into the glass. The tinkling sound set off a dog barking in another part of the house.

'My wife's pet. A temperance dog. He barks whenever I have a drink. I am convinced he is the reincarnation of Savonarola. One day I will strangle him,' said Soares, with an amiability that belied his stated intention.

'I heard that.'

Katarina was standing in the doorway, holding the object of her husband's ghoulish humour, a small, hairy dog no bigger than a rat. She was wearing a blue and yellow floral dress, white sandals and a scarf tied pirate-fashion around her head.

Both men rose.

'Mr Brant,' she said, acknowledging Ezra's presence.

'Good afternoon, Mrs Soares.'

'Will you join us for a drink, my dear?' asked her husband.

'You know the doctor said no alcohol.'

'Ah. Yes. No alcohol, no cigarettes. The life of a nun. Come and sit by me.'

Katarina looked significantly at Ezra who caught her meaning. She had been smoking against her doctor's orders, behind her husband's back. This was not the time to return her lighter.

Soares smiled at his wife and patted the cushion next to him. Katarina bent down and placed the dog with infinite care on the polished oak floor. It immediately urinated. Katarina gave a little cry and called for a maid, avoiding her husband's eyes. An expression of amused exasperation passed over Soares' face. He turned to Ezra.

'I was telling you about Coteiro, Mr Brant. For thirteen generations my family has farmed this land. It is in our blood. The sweat of our bodies has watered it and seen it flourish. Our will is as hard as the rocks we have had to break to plant our vines. Naturally, we will fight to retain what is ours.'

A maid appeared with a mop and pail. Her arrival was swift enough to suggest to Ezra that the dog's toilet habits were well-known to the staff.

'What happens if the courts find in favour of the Sykes family?' asked Ezra.

'There is justice in Portugal,' replied Soares enigmatically.

Katarina crossed the room and sat next to her husband, her hands folded in her lap. She looked pale and tired. Soares placed a proprietary hand on her thigh and continued talking.

'We have been in litigation for several years. In the meantime I continue to work the vineyard.'

The feud over the vineyard between the Soares and Sykes families reminded Ezra of another vineyard situation miles away in Lebanon. At Château Musar in the Bekaa Valley, Serge Hochar risked life and limb to bring in his harvest during the Lebanese War. In addition to Nature's depredations he had to put up with Syrian tanks and Israeli jets.

'When will you pick it?' asked Ezra, knowing that the other vineyards in the valley were already being harvested.

'Soon.'

He wondered if Soares was aware of the scope of the celebration Matthew Sykes had planned. No doubt his workers had informed him of the marquee being erected in the newly contoured vineyard.

'My husband likes to leave the grapes hanging for a long time,' interjected Katarina and a look passed between them that suggested the statement carried other nuances.

'Come, I would like to show you around,' said Soares.

He rose and put the whisky he had barely touched on the glass coffee table in front of him. The heavy circular slab of glass was supported by the highly polished root of an old vine artfully cut to balance its weight. Ezra took a last sip of his Highland Park and placed the glass beside his host's.

'Would you like to accompany us?' Soares asked his wife. She shook her head.

'I will ask Maria to prepare some food for our guest.'

★ ★ ★

The sun was blinding as they stepped outside. Ezra could feel the heat of the gravel stones through the leather soles of his shoes. Soares led him down a path through a line of chestnut trees.

'Tell me,' said Ezra, 'what do you know of Baron de Forrester?'

'There is an English firm, Offley Forrester, now owned by St Raphael, the French aperitif people. Baron de Forrester was a painter and a photographer. In fact, he painted my ancestor, Jorge Bernardo Soares who was a general in

169

Dom Pedro's army during the Civil War. It was a great pity he was drowned in the Douro.'

'Do you still have the portrait?'

'Yes, of course. It is hanging in my dining room.'

Ezra felt a growing sense of excitement. Joseph James Forrester was beginning to take shape as a person for him. He felt a strange sense of the man's presence here and he had an overwhelming urge to take out the letters from his jacket pocket, to sit under the shade of a chestnut tree and read them.

'Do you know where the portrait was painted? Was it here at the quinta?'

'Yes, of course. For a while Dona Antonia Adelaide Ferreira owned this property but my family still managed it. The Baron was her great friend and he would stay here on his trips up the Douro when he was making his map. You have seen his map?'

'Yes. At the Factory House.'

'Ah, the Factory House,' said Soares.

Ezra detected a note of sneering envy in his tone.

'You mean Forrester would have slept here?'

'Yes.'

'Are there any references to him? Letters, perhaps, or a diary?

'There were letters. My father showed them to me once. But I have no idea where they are now. Maybe he is in the guest book. It is a family tradition. We have volumes going back many years. We will check in the library.'

'The story I've been told is that he drowned because his boots filled with water and he was weighed down by his money belt.'

'Yes, I have heard this. My grandfather told me stories of the rapids before they used dynamite to open the gorge. As a child I remember the *rabelos* sailing downriver before they built the dam at Carrapatelo.'

'It must have been a magnificent sight.'

Ezra pictured in his mind's eye the flat-bottomed boats with their bosomy, square sails, loaded three tiers high with pipes of port, low in the water. Their four-man crews slept on board for three nights during the journey west, subsisting on dried cod, suckling pig, bread and oranges as they negotiated the treacherous river to its mouth at Oporto.

'There is poetry too in the hydroelectric dams they have built, my friend. Cathedrals in concrete. You must see them. That is progress. The modern Portugal. We must move with the times, no?'

As if on cue, they had arrived within sight of the gleaming stainless steel tanks that were such an eyesore when viewed from the valley below. Four of them stood like the sentinels of some extra-terrestrial colonizing force, guarding the savage landscape. What Ezra had not expected were the ten breast-shaped storage tanks that nestled behind them, each covered with white plaster.

'We call them *mamas*. Boobs,' said Soares, and he moved his hands as if he were testing the weight of melons.

They climbed a set of stone steps to another building on higher ground screened from below by a row of cypress trees. It looked like a large white warehouse with a red-tiled roof similar to the lodges he had seen in Vila Nova de Gaia. On the left was a concrete pad where a truck had drawn up. On its flatbed were two large, rectangular steel containers piled high with grape bunches. The driver and one of Soares' workers were tipping the first of the containers into a V-shaped metal trough. At the bottom was a long revolving screw which would move the grapes into the cylindrical crusher-destemmer machine. By centrifugal force the stalks would be removed to cut down the bitter tannins in the wine.

'The grape juice and skins are pumped automatically into our autovinifiers,' said Soares.

Inside the building there was none of the romance that characterized the lagares of Quinta do Santo Pedro. It looked more like a nuclear power plant. The rows of newly installed double-jacketed stainless steel tanks, the heat exchangers, the pumps, the filtering machines and the snaking plastic tubes gave the winery a futuristic look. All the equipment was shiny and new.

Lights had been strategically placed to illuminate the tanks. Someone had set them up to take photographs. White mesh screens, positioned in front of them, cut down the reflections from the shiny metal.

'We are making a brochure,' said Soares, tapping the side of the tank nearest him. 'In five languages, including Japanese. Our business is international.'

'Who's your photographer?' asked Ezra.

'He is here somewhere. An American. You will meet him.'

'I think we've already met,' said Ezra.

'I don't think so.'

The voice came from behind him. Ezra turned.

'Ah, Ralph, this is Ezra Brant, from Canada. Ralph is your neighbour in Los Angeles. He lives near Hollywood.'

The two men shook hands and eyed each other. The photographer wore army denims and a light, sleeveless waistcoat covered with pockets. A light meter hung from a black ribbon around his neck. His blond hair was cropped close to the scalp.

His skin was bronzed from the sun and his blue eyes darted restlessly as if following the flight of some threatening wasp. His handshake was firm and his flesh as cold as a reptile's.

'Ralph Maddox. Pleasure,' he said.

'Hi,' said Ezra. 'How's the story going for *National Geographic*?'

'What?'

'I thought you had an assignment from *National Geographic*.'

Maddox frowned, then shrugged.

'Whatever.'

He knelt down and unzipped a large black camera bag, and took out a Nikon body and then fished inside for a lens.

'Boy, I could really use you on this trip,' said Ezra.

'Yeah,' said Maddox, still rooting through his bag.

'I have a Nikon too.'

'Good camera.'

'Come,' said Soares. 'We will leave Ralph to finish his work. I pay him by the hour.'

He put an arm around Ezra's shoulder and led him towards the door.

They sat down in the living room again. In their absence two sets of glasses had been placed on the glass coffee table. Next to them was a press kit, several bottles of port of differing ages and a decanter.

'Now you must taste what we do at Quinta do Coteiro,' said Soares as he poured a small measure of each bottle into the glasses.

Katarina was nowhere to be seen but the evanescent fragrance of her perfume still hung in the room and Ezra wished that she would return. As if Soares could read his mind, he said:

'My wife has prepared the documentation for you.'

Ezra picked up the glossy folder and opened it. Inside was a metal pin with the company crest, a hawk with wings spread. The same logo was repeated on the neck labels of the bottles. Set into the left-hand side of the folder was a single piece of paper. It was a tasting sheet for the wines Ezra was about to try. His name had been printed across the top: 'Tasting for Ezra Brant of Quinta do Coteiro ports.' It gave the date and technical details on each wine — the name, vintage, degree of alcohol, total acidity, residual sugar and the grape varieties from which they were made. Each port was a blend of Touriga Nacional, Touriga Francesa, Tinta Roriz and Tinta Cão.

Slotted into the right-hand side was a press release that gave a history of the firm and behind it a glossy booklet that featured photos of the different wines artistically arranged among old clocks.

Alvaro Soares noticed that Ezra was pausing at the photos of the wine bottles.

'Those are only our ports. We have another booklet for our table wines.'

'I was interested in the clocks,' said Ezra.

'Ah. That is my collection. I have a man whose job it is only to wind them each day and clean them.'

'It must be very valuable,' said Ezra.

'I have it insured at Lloyd's of London for £2.5 million. We will start with our simple ruby port.'

As Soares poured an ounce into their glasses Ezra studied the booklet. There were photos of the new double-jacketed tanks which made him wonder why Soares would need a new brochure. He checked the back for the photography credit. Rodriego Gedes from a studio in Oporto.

Katarina arrived with a tray bearing mineral water, glasses, a glass bowl with small cubes of bread and a platter of cheese and nuts and a variety of finger foods.

'Thank you, my dear,' said Soares with elaborate courtesy as Katarina set the tray down.

A thin film of perspiration glistened on her forehead although the air-conditioning rendered the living room decidedly chilly.

'The British would serve you Stilton with these ports. They like the contrast of the salty blue cheese and the sweet wine. I prefer complementary flavours and that is why I serve Serra, Portugal's most famous cheese. Will you join us, my dear?'

Katarina shook her head.

'If Mr Brant will excuse me, I will lie down.'

The two men stood up as she left the room. When she was out of earshot, Soares said, 'She is beautiful, no?'

Ezra nodded. She was very beautiful. He wondered how much Soares had insured her for.

★ ★ ★

Quinta do Santo Pedro appeared deserted when Ezra arrived back in the jeep. He parked in the shade of the horse chestnut tree and pulled open the gate. It creaked on its hinges causing a couple of birds to rise in panic from the tree.

The late afternoon sun was low in the sky and the earth was giving off the heat that it had accumulated during the day. Soares had not provided a spit bucket. Under other circumstances Ezra would have asked for something to spit into but for some reason he had not wanted to be patronized by his host who swallowed each wine they had tried together.

The wines themselves were competently made but overall they lacked style. They were commercial and priced to sell, as Soares had explained. The only one that Ezra felt he could recommend was the twenty-year-old tawny. A beautifully balanced wine with a nutty, dried-raisin taste that lingered on the palate. It had been made by Soares' father two months before he died. The old man must have had a premonition of his death, thought Ezra, and wanted to leave behind a testimony to his life.

Ezra looked around the courtyard. The only sound was the plashing of the fountain. He moved inside the house. Someone had placed a guest book on the table in the hall. It had not been there when he left and was open at a new page. He picked it up and turned the page back, curious to see who had been there before him. He recognized the name of Sykes' Chicago-based importer. There were a couple of names with English addresses and comments which suggested they were friends ('Heavenly picnic but where was the champers?') and then he came across an entry at the end of the page before the fresh one where the book lay open that made him do a double-take.

Printed in a spiky hand was the name and Lisbon address of Amanda Sykes. In the 'Comments' column she had written, 'I *am* a guest after all.'

The entry was dated four days before his arrival.

There was something very sad behind the irony of the remark. A wife who had grown tired of her marriage after twenty-eight years, who came to the quinta for the last time and considered herself a guest rather than a member of the family. He remembered Matthew's words: 'She hates the Douro and has sworn never to set foot in Santo Pedro again.'

'I left the book out for you to sign.'

Helen's voice startled him. She was standing in the corridor leading to the kitchen, a glass in her hand.

'Would you like an iced tea? It's very refreshing on such a hot day.'

'No, thank you. I was just thinking of something witty to write. Maybe I'll make up a limerick.'

'I love limericks. I was brought up on Edward Lear. Once I could recite 'The Owl and the Pussy Cat' in its entirety. That was my party piece.'

'Mine was 'The Shooting of Dan McGrew'.'

'I'm not familiar with it.'

'A ballad by Robert Service, the Canadian equivalent of Sir Henry Newbolt. 'There's a breathless hush in the close tonight, ten to make and a match to win.' '

'I remember that.'

'It always struck me as the most British of poems. Not very good but somehow it captured the essence of being English. 'Play up, play up and play the game.' '

'You haven't lived in England lately,' said Helen. 'It's got more to do with soccer hooligans and queer-bashing.'

She looked as if she were about to take flight. Ezra wanted to keep her talking.

'What happened to Matthew and Luke?'

'They went down to the police station with those men. They shouldn't be long.'

'On second thoughts,' said Ezra, 'I think I will have that iced tea. On one condition.'

'What's that?'

'You sit down in the living room with me and keep me company.'

She smiled at him with her long horsy face and her large red hands fluttered to her cheeks as if to wipe away the momentary expression of pleasure and confusion.

'I'll just drop this off in my room and meet you down here. Okay?'

Helen nodded and patted her hair.

He deposited the Quinta do Coteiro press kit out of sight in his suitcase, ran some cold water from the jug over his hands, dried them and returned downstairs. By the time he arrived Helen was already seated. She had placed his glass of iced tea on a small lace doily on the coffee table adjacent to the sofa. She had seated herself across the table from him in a cane chair.

'Hot, isn't it?' she said, fanning herself with a handkerchief. 'I don't know if I will ever get used to this heat.'

'Never this hot in London, eh?'

'I don't know London that well. We used to — I used to go up there for the shows. Shopping at Harrods, that sort of thing.'

'May I ask you a personal question? If I'm prying just tell me to back off,' said Ezra.

He could see her stiffen visibly as if a tyrannical school-teacher had yelled at her to sit up straight.

'That all depends,' she said, spreading her fingers along the edge of the coffee table.

'I noticed from the guest book that your aunt Amanda stayed here just before I arrived.'

'Yes.'

'I find it really weird that she should sign the guest book in her own home.'

'Oh, that's Auntie Amanda. She has a very bizarre sense of humour.'

'Your uncle told me they were separated. That she would never set foot here again.'

'He told you that!'

'Yes.'

Helen raised her eyebrows and pulled the hem of her dress over her knees.

'That's not at all like Matthew. Talking about his private life to . . . '

She hesitated, searching for the right word to describe Ezra. Not finding one she cleared her throat and continued.

'He's one of those Englishmen who use joviality as a mask . . . I'm just surprised, that's all. Him telling you that.'

'Did they quarrel?'

He could see the woman was becoming agitated.

'All married people quarrel.'

'Yes, but there's something very final about saying you'll never set foot in your family home again.'

'They have a flat in Lisbon.'

'But this is where they lived and I don't see any photos of Amanda around. Lots of Matthew.'

'Sometimes I think Matthew is a misogynist. But he has always been very kind to me.'

She looked away as if she had said too much, taking refuge in her iced tea.

'Have you ever tried that with Scotch?'

asked Ezra, filling the silence between them.

'Iced tea?'

'Sure. My father was a doctor. He used to prescribe it before it became politically incorrect for doctors to suggest alcohol to their patients. Do you have any whisky around?'

'There's a decanter in the dining room.'

'Then why don't we try it?'

Unsure, Helen rose and moved to the door that connected the living and dining rooms. The way she walked suggested to Ezra that she wanted there to be no movement of her clothes. Nothing to suggest the shape of the body beneath the light cotton of her dress. Ezra could see the impression the cane chair had left on her skin between her shoulder blades. Or was it something other than the pressure of her back against the chair that had made those marks?

She returned with a crystal decanter and removed the top.

'How much should I put in?' she asked, bending over his glass.

'A couple of ounces.'

'Here goes. Whoops.'

'That's fine. Thank you.'

She poured her own glass and took a sip.

'Mmmm. That's really quite good. What do you call it?'

'My father used to call it 'The Prescription'. 'I'm going to give you the prescription,' he'd say to his patients, especially the old ladies. 'And you'll be as right as rain in the morning.' '

Helen laughed.

'That's the first time I've seen you really laugh,' said Ezra.

'I suppose I haven't had much to laugh about lately,' she said.

'It must be very lonely for you here. It's pretty remote.'

'I need the peace.'

She looked wistfully towards the window with its view of the distant purple hills across the Douro.

'Last night I went for a walk and I saw you in the chapel,' said Ezra. 'You were praying. It seemed to me you were crying.'

'I — perhaps it was the light. Candlelight can make the eyes glisten,' said Helen, locking her fingers together.

'Sometimes it's good to talk about things to a sympathetic stranger.'

She looked at him as if she was seeing him for the first time. She tilted her head, weighing his invitation.

'I was upset, that's all. All these strange things going on around here,' she said. 'This event, it makes me nervous. There will be so many people coming in a couple of days. Every bed in the quinta will be occupied. We've hired extra staff to help entertain them but ultimately it's my responsibility as chatelaine.'

Ezra could tell she was not yet ready to confide in him as her uncle Matthew had done.

'You wear a wedding ring, Helen. Is your husband in England?'

'I'm divorced,' she said, with finality.

'So am I,' said Ezra. 'Not much fun is it.'

'No. But it's better than being married to a man who beats you.'

The marks down her back. The legacy

of an abusive marriage?

'Is that why you left England?'

'The family decided it would be best for me to come here. Uncle Matthew needed someone to run the place when Aunt . . . Oh my goodness, I do believe this whisky is going to my head! I hardly ever drink spirits, you know.'

'The Prescription's working.'

Helen laughed.

'How long have you been here?'

'This will be my third harvest. I arrived just as they were picking the 1995 vintage. Well, I really must get back to work, Mr Brant.'

'Ezra.'

The whisky had brought some colour to her cheeks and made her lose some of the anxiety that coiled her up like a watch spring.

'I think I hear Matthew's car.'

Helen stood up, glass of iced tea in her hand.

'One last thing,' said Ezra. 'When your aunt stayed here the other night which room did she sleep in?'

'The one you're staying in.'

'And when did she leave?'

He could hear Matthew and Luke talking as they crossed the courtyard outside.

'Actually she was here for three days. She left the morning you arrived. I hardly had time to prepare the room.'

Ezra turned the information over in his mind as the voices grew louder. Amanda Sykes had not slept in her husband's bed yet she had stayed for three nights at the quinta. Matthew had told him over coffee at the outdoor restaurant on the Cais dos Guindais in Oporto that his wife had sworn never to set foot in Santo Pedro again. That statement could only have been made after a fight they had had at the quinta the night before he arrived. Yet Matthew was in Oporto the next day and according to Helen he stayed at his club. Or could the argument that had caused her to utter such an ultimatum have been between Amanda and Luke? Yet Matthew himself knew she had spoken those words the very next day. Luke could have phoned his father that night or the next morning after Amanda had left the quinta and told him about their quarrel and his mother's sworn intention; but if it was Luke who had been the cause of Amanda's anger, surely her husband would have tried to play the role of peacemaker in the family and interceded with her. Unless Matthew was sure the break was final he would not have confided the fact to me, Ezra reasoned. So the fight must have been between husband and wife.

What had precipitated it and had it anything to do with the 'accidents' that kept occurring around the property?

And then there was the question of the snake. Perhaps it was meant to kill Amanda Sykes, or at least frighten *her* away rather than him. But Helen and Luke and even Matthew must have known that Amanda would not be sleeping in that bed last night. Whoever put the snake there was not a member of the family.

Matthew Sykes came striding into the living room, followed by Luke. Both were serious expressions.

'Ezra. I'm glad you're back. We've had

some unfortunate news. Our farm manager, Albino Sousa, is dead. His body was found floating in the Douro this morning.'

Helen Sykes collapsed into the chair she had occupied and began to tremble.

'Oh God, this is too much,' she murmured. 'Just too much.'

Ezra tried to recall Albino Sousa to mind. He could only remember the man's scowling face, staring at him across the lagar and angrily confronting him for his lapse of etiquette. He had seen the farm manager again last night at the cockfight before the police arrived. He felt strangely moved by the news of Sousa's death as if he had foretold it or had read a newspaper account of an accident and experienced that generalized sense of loss when the life of a stranger is cut short.

'How did it happen?' he asked.

'The police are not sure. They think he must have stumbled while walking along the river. They suspect he might have been drinking. There was a gash on his forehead. Their theory is he probably tripped, struck his head on a rock and fell in.'

'At least the harvest is all but done,' said Luke.

'Luke! How could you?' exclaimed Helen.

Luke shrugged.

'The police asked me to identify the body,' said Matthew. 'Poor fellow. He didn't have much of a life. It was one thing after another for that family. First his eldest daughter lost a child last Christmas. Then his brother Luis got pinned under a tractor that rolled over on him. And now this.'

'When do they think it happened?' asked Ezra.

'Their forensic people said it was early this morning.'

'We'll have to get Vasco to supervise the picking of the lower vineyard,' said Luke.

'Yes, go and attend to it, will you. I'll have to visit the family and offer my condolences,' said his father. 'What was his wife's name?'

'Maria,' said Helen.

'I'll be in the warehouse if you need me,' said Luke.

He exchanged a significant look with his father.

'Yes,' said Sykes. 'Under the circumstances it would be better if you remained here.'

'Would you mind if I came with you?' asked Ezra.

'My dear fellow, I'd be only too delighted to have company. It's not going to be much fun for either of us, I'm afraid. The Portuguese take death very seriously. I shall go and change into something suitable. I suppose you don't travel with a black tie?'

'No, the closest I get is a dark blue with gold stripes.'

'Helen will rustle you up a black armband. I'll see you down here in fifteen minutes. Is that all right?'

*　*　*

When Matthew Sykes returned he had changed from his three-piece linen suit into a grey flannel one, far too heavy for the temperature outside. He wore a black tie and with his gaunt, sunken face he resembled an undertaker on a cold call.

'We'll take the Mercedes,' he said. 'The family will appreciate that. Adds a touch of solemnity to the occasion, don't you agree, rather than rolling up in a jeep?'

'I suppose it does,' replied Ezra, fixing the black armband Helen had found for him to his left bicep.

'They put a lot of store by the little things,' said Sykes as they drove down the hill.

Ezra debated whether he should tell Sykes about seeing Albino Sousa at the cockfight but he decided against it since it might implicate the smiling Vasco Gedes in an illegal activity his employer would probably frown upon. Instead he recounted the incident in the lagar.

'Luke told me about that,' said Sykes. 'All grist to the mill for your book, what?'

They drove in silence for a moment.

'Was there a death certificate?' asked Ezra.

'I imagine there would be one. Why do you ask?'

'I'm just curious as to why the police would assume it was an accident. Where did they find his body?'

'A little downstream from one of Coteiro's vineyards.'

'Have they talked to Alvaro Soares?'

'They'll probably talk to all the quinta owners along this stretch of the Douro. And they may want to talk to you too.'

It had not occurred to Ezra that he would become implicated in the death of Sykes' farm manager. Perhaps someone had told the police of his confrontation with Albino Sousa in the lagar, making more of it than was the case.

They had arrived at the main road and Sykes turned in the direction Ezra had walked the previous night when he had been picked up by Katarina Soares.

'It must have occurred to you that Albino Sousa's death could be part of what's been going on. Just the latest event in the chain of incidents to disturb your celebration.'

'I had thought of that. But the other things were just minor irritants. If I believed that people's lives were at risk

I would call the whole thing off. It's not worth it. Vainglorious really, when you put it in perspective. Besides, it's a bit late.'

'I don't call being shot at a minor irritant, Matthew, and as for finding a snake in my bed . . . '

'I knew we had snakes in the vineyard but why the devil would it be in the house?'

'And climb the stairs and get into my bed.'

'You poor fellow. It must have given you a terrible turn.'

'Well, I've had better nights.'

'I'll speak to Helen about it. If someone's been playing practical jokes there'll be hell to pay.'

'Tell me about Helen.'

Sykes glanced at him, the first time he had taken his eyes off the road.

'Interested are you?'

'Just curious.'

Ezra felt himself flushing and was surprised by his own reaction. He felt protective towards Helen, a vague sexual attraction as well perhaps. More of a reflex emotion. The need for a divorced man on his own to be found desirable by a woman. They were both wounded. He had found solace in his work and she in escape from an abusive relationship.

'My niece was married to a major in the Welch Fusiliers. The chap had a drinking problem. Thought he'd died and gone to heaven when he married into a port family. He was an avid rugby fan. More of a fanatic, really. Whenever Wales lost he'd come home and beat his wife. It was all right in the early days of their marriage when Wales had a good team, but in the last five years . . . '

'The marks on her back. Did he do that?'

'With a fly rod.'

'A fly rod?'

'If his dinner was not prepared when he came home from one of his binges he would take the rod to her.'

'What happened?'

'He came back one night after an international at Twickenham. Wales had lost against England. Drunk out of his mind with a stranger. A drinking partner he'd latched onto in a pub. When he left the room to go to the toilet this fellow tried to rape Helen on the kitchen table. She was screaming for help apparently and when Hugh came back and saw what was going on he did nothing. He just stood there laughing. Before this animal could do anything he passed out, thank God. Helen took a knife from the kitchen drawer and stabbed Hugh in the stomach.'

'Did she kill him?'

'No. He spent a night in hospital, a few stitches. My brother John went to see his commanding officer. The regiment would not allow Hugh to press charges. For her own safety the family decided Helen should leave England and come here. She's like my right hand now. But I will ask her about the snake.'

Ezra looked out towards the river. The sun was low, casting the shadow of the hills over half its expanse. A motorboat was moving swiftly up river, bouncing off the surface of the water and sending out a creamy wake.

There is a difference, he was thinking,

between finding a harmless grass snake in your bedclothes and a poisonous viper — a distinction that Matthew Sykes did not seem to grasp. A grass snake was a practical joke, a horned viper was attempted murder. He decided to take the conversation in another direction.

'I read that they used to have cockfights in Portugal. Is that true?'

'Yes. It's illegal now, of course, but it still goes on in the rural areas. The Portuguese are great gamblers.'

What nation isn't these days, thought Ezra. And most loved blood sports. The number of pubs named 'The Bear' was living testimony to the amount of bear-baiting that went on in eighteenth-century England. To say nothing of that inexplicable desire of upper-class Englishmen and women to mount a horse in order to chase a fox and watch it be torn apart by a pack of dogs. He left the thought unspoken as another came into his head.

'I imagine they'd get pretty attached to a favourite bird and if it got killed . . . '

Ezra's mind was working through the

possible reasons why Albino Sousa might have met his death. He felt in the core of his being that this was no accident. There was something in the man's face, a venom made flesh, that had marked him for violent death. And not by accident. Some men have the gallows written across their foreheads; Albino Sousa had murder victim emblazoned across his. Perhaps he would understand more when he had seen the man's home.

Sykes had turned off onto a side road that snaked up the hill between an established vineyard and one that had been restructured into a large banked-up hillside that sloped down to where the road came closest to the river bank.

'That's our new vineyard,' said Sykes, proudly. 'We'll be planting in the early spring. We'll use the double Guyot pruning system, leaving three or five eyes which will give us eight to twelve canes. Look! Do you see that bird, the small black one with the white tail feathers? We call it the port wine bird. Actually it's the Black Wheateater. You find it everywhere in the Upper Douro. The little bugger feeds on the best wine grapes.'

Ezra was not looking at the bird. He was marvelling at the spectacle of the vineyard with its perfect exposure to the sun.

'That's a beautiful sight,' he said.

'Yes, that's the future of Santo Pedro. All our capital is tied up in that. You see how close we are to the river. There's an old Portuguese saying, 'The wine to be good must hear the creak of the tiller.' Nowadays it's the roar of the speedboat, unfortunately.'

They were climbing steeply now. The last rays of the sun turned the camel-coloured outcrops of granite to gold. Ezra could see above him a small church with a cluster of red-tiled houses around it.

'The village of Cotas,' remarked Sykes. 'This is where he lived. I offered him a room at the quinta rent-free but he wanted to stay in his village. He used to cycle every day to our quinta, up and down these hills. Must have had leg muscles of steel.'

The narrow main street was deserted apart from a couple of dogs growling at each other over a bone.

Ezra wondered what Albino Sousa had been doing, walking down by the river in the early hours of the morning, drunk. It was a long way from his house. How did he get to the cockfight? Did he cycle with his bird in a sack or did a neighbour give him a lift?

Sykes drove slowly along the street studying the houses.

'That's it.'

The door was open and a woman dressed in black was going in with a tray covered with a dishcloth. Sykes drew the car up outside the house and parked in the shade of its whitewashed wall.

They both had to stoop under the lintel to get through the door. The room they found themselves in was full of women in black dresses and headscarves seated on chairs around the walls. In the centre, set on two trestles, was an ornate mahogany coffin with gleaming metal handles. Tall candles in wrought-iron holders burned at each end of the coffin and at the top end stood a large brass crucifix. Floral wreaths and flowers arranged in the shape of palm trees had been stacked around the coffin. Lilies, gladioli, roses.

Inside, his head resting on an embroidered pillow, lay Albino Sousa, dressed in his Sunday suit, a white shirt and black tie. His hands lay crossed on his chest. No amount of scrubbing by the woman who had laid him out could wash away the dirt ingrained under his nails or encrusted in the lines of his pallid fingers. His black hair had been combed and pomaded to a flat shiny helmet, all the blacker for the straight white line of his parting and the whiteness of the coffin's billowing satin interior. His feet, encased in brown shoes, were remarkably small. Even in death he wore the same truculent frown Ezra had experienced in life.

He could make out the wound to Sousa's left temple, a slight indentation that had been artfully covered with makeup.

Ezra noticed a small table set to one side covered with a lace cloth. On it was a framed black and white photograph of Albino Sousa in soccer gear, hands on hips, a silver whistle in his mouth and his cleated boot resting on a soccer ball. The frame was draped in black ribbon. Also on the table were a variety of objects, obviously treasured artefacts of the deceased — his silver whistle hanging from a plaited lanyard, his pruning knife, a gold St Christopher medallion.

What intrigued Ezra was the presence on the table of a wooden box unnervingly mimicking in miniature the casket that stood in the middle of the room. The 'body' inside this box was an unopened bottle of Royal Lochnagar Selected Reserve single malt whisky. Even across the room Ezra could recognize the famous blue and gold label. Glued to the inside panel of the hinged lid was the whisky's certificate of authenticity and the number of the bottle.

Ezra knew of Lochnagar, a small distillery on the River Dee in the eastern Highlands. It was located near Balmoral Castle and its enterprising owner had invited Queen Victoria and Prince Albert to visit when they purchased Balmoral in 1848. As a result Lochnagar became a royal supplier and Queen Victoria, who had already been responsible for the creation of the champagne coupe (designed specifically to take the bubbles out of champagne and thereby reduce flatulence) proceeded to desecrate two more of the world's finest beverages by adding Lochnagar malt whisky to her claret.

But how did a Portuguese farm manager who never left his village come to possess a bottle of one of Scotland's rarest malt whiskies?

There could only have been one source. He got it from a collector of single malts. Alvaro Soares.

What service had Albino Sousa performed that merited such a gift, one so precious the recipient had not even opened it and thought so highly of it that his wife displayed it along with his other cherished objects next to his coffin?

Or did the man steal it from Soares' house? Either way he would have had contact of some kind with the quinta owner and the enemy of his own employer.

He wondered if Matthew Sykes knew

of a connection between his farm manager and his litigious neighbour. This was not the time to find out and perhaps it was a piece of information best kept to himself for the time being.

He watched Sykes walk up to the woman who sat nearest the coffin, running rosary beads through her fingers. She had the weathered, leathery face of someone who spends their life outdoors in the wind. She looked as if she were sixty years old but was probably only forty, a squat, heavy woman whose loss had turned her face into that of a sad clown. There was a low moaning sound that seemed to emanate from no one in particular but rose like vapour as an expression of the collective sense of grief.

Sykes bent down and spoke quietly to Sousa's widow. She looked fearful at first and then she smiled wanly at him. She rose, leading him by the hand to the centre of the room.

Ezra watched Sykes as he bent at the waist to peer into the coffin. He recoiled momentarily, shook his head and murmured, 'What a pity.'

The woman gave a short sob and sucked in her trembling lips as she tried to restrain her anguish. The sound of her grief set off the keening wail of the other women. The woman took Sykes by the hand again and led him to a doorway on the right of the coffin. Sykes motioned for Ezra to follow him. The woman preceded them into a smaller room which was dominated by a large table filled with plates of food. A large bowl stood in the middle of the table. It appeared to be dried chestnut soup surrounded by loaves of bread. There were grapes and peaches and individual bowls of custard cream. At the end of the table was an assortment of glasses and tumblers set on a wicker tray on which stood several unlabelled bottles of port.

A man, dressed in a tight-fitting blue suit stained with food, was hovering over the dishes helping himself liberally to slices of ham, roast kid and meat loaf. When he saw Sykes he smiled, revealing a mouthful of food. His head was shaking from side to side. He held his plate in both hands and did a shuffling dance as if he wanted to offer it to them.

'Luis Sousa, Albino's brother,' Sykes whispered to Ezra. 'The one who had the tractor accident.'

Sykes patted the man on the shoulder as one might pet an overly affectionate dog who approached for attention.

The woman made a clicking sound with her tongue and the man brushed imaginary flies from his face.

'Mama.'

The voice of a young woman behind them made both men turn.

She must have been in her early twenties. Her hands were clasped protectively over her stomach. She wore a black shawl over her head, a black skirt and a purple satinette blouse buttoned at the throat with a cameo brooch.

To Ezra's eyes, she was as beautiful as Katarina Soares only much younger. She wore no make-up, but the high cheekbones, the brightness of her eyes and the natural redness of her lips compelled attention.

With the smattering of Portuguese he had picked up, Ezra understood her to say that the priest had arrived. She smiled wanly at Sykes whom she recognized and lowered her eyes under Ezra's appreciative gaze.

Her mother picked up two plates and handed them to Ezra and Sykes before leaving to greet the priest.

'Eat something, even if you don't feel hungry,' said Sykes.

Luis continued to dance around them, begging for attention.

'Who was that?' asked Ezra.

'That's his younger daughter, Aurelia.'

'She looked pregnant.'

'She is.'

'But she wasn't wearing a wedding ring.'

Sykes looked at him with pursed lips.

'That's one of the problems. She's going to have a baby. Sousa locked her in her room until she told him who the father was. He wanted to force him to marry her to save the family's honour. When the man refused he went for him with his pruning knife. Nearly cut off his thumb.'

'Luke?'

'What makes you think it was Luke?'

'The scar on his thumb and something you said before we left the quinta. 'Under the circumstances it would be better if you remained here.' '

'Yes,' said Sykes, wearily. 'Much to my shame, it was my son. The damned young fool.'

'Yet you didn't fire Sousa even after that.'

'No. He was a good worker and a little blood-letting satisfied honour all round.'

★ ★ ★

Sykes and he stayed for a half hour at the dead man's house and his wife was extravagant in her display of gratitude for their visit there. At the door she took Sykes' hand and pressed it to her lips, a gesture that embarrassed the man terribly.

'She's a very brave woman,' said Sykes, in the car.

They drove back to the quinta in silence, each cocooned in his own thoughts. He wondered how Sykes had handled the news that Luke had had an affair with the daughter of an employee and might well have been killed by her outraged father. Now that man was dead, supposedly drowned in the river after a fall that had knocked him unconscious. Luke had not been at home last night. Had he waited all this time to revenge himself on Albino Sousa for the scar he would carry to his grave? The young man might have spent the night at the guest cottage. The perfume on the pillow suggested he might not have been alone.

If only Ezra could find out the approximate time of Sousa's death. Sykes had said the police might want to question him. He could learn more about how the farm manager died if they did call him in.

'Tomorrow we'll go and have a look at the site for the marquee,' said Sykes. 'They should have it up and running by then. See you for a drink before dinner. I'll have Gertrudes ring the gong. How's that?'

'Terrific. I think I'll get down to a bit of writing.'

Before he set up his laptop on the desk in his bedroom Ezra glanced nervously at the bed. In case the snake had taken a liking to it he reached for the long wooden rod the maids used to open and close the shutters and poked tentatively at the counterpane with it. There was no movement from under the blankets. He slid the rod between the sheets and with a pendulum-like motion began to sweep the bed, praying that no one would walk in on him during the de-snaking operation. To his great relief he found nothing.

He opened his file on Forrester and began reading the notes.

Among his other talents, Forrester was an accomplished artist. Apart from his detailed topographical maps of the River Douro and the Wine District, he sketched and painted at a highly professional level.

He produced many sketches, drawings and photos of the region he loved which provided social historians with vivid records of the period.

He was also a recognized portrait

painter whose subjects included royalty and high society (viz. his painting of the Duke of Saldanha).

The maps, however, were his greatest legacy. The Oporto Town Council wrote a letter of congratulation to him in April 1843 following the publication of his map of the river from Spain to the Atlantic: 'The gigantic and well-executed task to which he had devoted himself, a task which confers much honour and distinction upon him by the proof which he has given of his talents and extraordinary skill; and from which must result great advantages to Science, but more especially to the Portuguese nation, whose prosperity the author has so much at heart.'

It had taken him twelve years and a huge personal investment to complete the project. He would venture into the interior alone for days on end, at great personal risk, taking readings of angles by chains of triangles which he would check for accuracy using a theodolite. (He wrote to his daughters in England: 'My works were examined by a Professor of Mathematics of the Royal Polytechnic Academy of this City (Oporto) and passed muster.')

Forrester gave the first copy of the printed map to King Ferdinand II who, in recognition of his achievement, ennobled him with a barony in 1855.

His most famous watercolour was painted in 1834 just after the Civil War. It depicts the Rua Nova dos Inglezes — the New Street of the English — with fifty-four prominent English and Portuguese merchants chatting in groups outside their offices. The original which used to hang in Offley Forrester's London offices was destroyed by fire during the Second World War. Happily, Forrester had sent the painting to England to be engraved so several copies survive . . .

Ezra's concentration was broken by the sound of a gong from below. Its eerie metallic note reverberated through the house, a mournful, visceral sound that he always associated with bad news.

He saved the material, shut down the computer and slid it into his suitcase. The echo of the gong had barely faded away when there was a knock at his door.

'Come in.'

Helen Sykes stood in the doorway. Her expression was conspiratorial and apologetic at the same time. She wore a different dress than the one he had seen her in earlier in the day — black and white stripes that made her look even taller than she was.

'Excuse me,' she said. 'I just wanted to call you down for drinks.'

'Yes,' said Ezra, 'I heard the gong.'

'The gong.'

She hovered in the doorway as if reluctant to leave. Sensing she had something to tell him he invited her in and closed the door.

'I wanted to apologize,' she began.

'For what?'

'Oh, burdening you with my problems. It's just that I don't have many people to talk to around here.'

'I'm delighted you did,' said Ezra. 'I'm a good listener.'

'Thank you.'

She made no move to leave.

'There is something else you wanted to say, wasn't there.'

'I — I was upset by Albino Sousa's death. I never liked the man but he has a family. A wife, two daughters. The younger, Aurelia, used to help out when we were entertaining.'

'Used to?'

'She can't any longer.'

'Why not?'

'Her father refused to let her come to the house. I used to teach her English. She had a natural ear for languages.'

'When you say help out, what do you mean? Serve at table, work in the kitchen?'

'No, she had a job as a chambermaid in the hotel at Pinhão. She cleaned the bedrooms, changed the beds. She was fast and efficient.'

'Could you talk to her?'

'Oh, yes. I don't know how much she

understood. You see, I don't speak Portuguese, apart from a few words. So I spoke to her in English as I would to a friend. And I liked looking at her. She is very beautiful.'

'Yes. I saw her at the wake.'

'Did you speak to her? Did she say anything?'

'No, I hardly met her. But her uncle was there.'

'Luis.'

'Yes.'

'Poor Luis.'

'What happened to him?'

'He was working in the new vineyard and his tractor turned over on him. He could have been crushed but he got wedged between two large rocks. It might have been better if he had died. He's a vegetable now. Matthew still supports him though.'

'When did it happen?'

'A few months ago. June I think. Yes, around flowering time. I think we'd better go down now. Matthew is a stickler for time.'

'One last question.'

Ezra reached into the pocket of his jacket and took out the gold wedding band. He held it out to her in the palm of his hand.

'Do you recognize this?'

Helen squinted myopically at the ring.

'Take it,' he said.

He barely felt the brush of her nails as she picked the ring from his hand. She held it up to the light and turned it in her fingers.

'Where did you get this?' she demanded.

'I found it last night. While I was treading grapes in the lagar I felt it with my toes.'

'You found it in the lagar!'

'Yes. Whose is it?'

Helen had turned pale.

'It's Auntie Amanda's wedding ring.'

'You said she left yesterday morning. Did she drive or did Vasco give her a lift to the station?'

'She must have driven because she came in her own car.'

'Did you see her leave the quinta?'

'No. I left early for the market. There's

219

a farmer's market in Pinhão.'

'Did she have breakfast?'

'She never eats breakfast.'

'Why don't you phone her in Lisbon and tell her you've found her ring?' said Ezra.

Helen moved from one foot to the other, obviously uncomfortable at the idea.

'I think you should give it to Matthew. After all, he gave it to her in the first place.'

She turned and walked swiftly from the room.

*　　*　　*

Matthew Sykes was on the telephone when Ezra descended the staircase. He was making notes on a pad and speaking in Portuguese. Ezra considered the best way to hand the wedding ring back to him. He would have to plead a lapse of memory for not having done it sooner.

The smell of roast lamb, rosemary and garlic wafted in from the kitchen. Ezra could see Luke sitting at the table in the courtyard, swatting flies with the flat of his hand.

'Do you speak English?' Sykes was asking into the receiver. 'Good, because he speaks no Portuguese . . . yes . . . yes . . . I'll tell him.'

'That was the police, Ezra. As I suspected, they would like to interview you.'

'Now?'

'You can slip down there and be back in time for dinner. It's merely a formality. They'll check your passport, ask you a few questions. The police station is just round the corner from the railway station in Pinhão. I'll get Vasco to drive you. We'll have a quick one while he brings the car around.'

Vasco was nervous. He talked to himself all the way into Pinhão. Instead of driving the Mercedes right up to the police station he parked a block away and pointed to the building.

Ezra understood the reason for his anxiety. Vasco had participated in the illegal cockfight and soon after its premature end his co-worker had been found drowned in the Douro. At least his bird had not been matched against Albino Sousa's. No doubt the police now had a list of all the spectators at the event and were interviewing them one by one.

'Are you going to wait here for me?' asked Ezra.

Vasco nodded and slumped down in his seat, pretending to sleep.

Ezra showed his passport to the officer at the desk and was ushered into a small waiting room, invited to sit and the door was closed behind him. The windows were closed and the atmosphere inside was stifling. Flies bounced against the window trying to escape death by sauna. He tried to lift the frame but it had been painted shut.

Ezra could feel the perspiration running down his body. He opened the door to try to get a crossdraught. He took off his jacket and hung it on the back of the chair, cranky now with the oven-like ambience. He looked around for something to read to take his mind off the heat. There was a poster on the wall with instructions on how to secure your house against burglars. Somebody had written graffiti in Portuguese in the margin and someone else had added under it, 'Ha, ha!'

He sat down and picked up the sole magazine on the table. There was a photo of the Benfica soccer team on the cover. He put it down again. He closed his eyes and thought about Toronto in January. The crunch of newly fallen snow under your boots; the needle-sharp air when you first step out in the mornings; icicles like stalactites glistening in the sun and the arctic wind that makes your eyes water and freezes the cheeks until you think they're burning.

Eventually he heard voices down the hall. He looked up and saw a short man in a white linen jacket escorting a woman to the entrance.

It was Katarina Soares. Her head was covered with a baseball cap worn over a silk kerchief knotted around her scalp.

So they're questioning her too, he thought. They must have found out she was at the cockfight.

Their eyes met and she registered

surprise. She inclined her head towards the street, signalling to him that she would wait for him outside. He nodded slightly and watched her step out into the sunshine. The man who accompanied her returned.

'Senhor Brant. My name is Cruz. Julio Francisco Cruz, detective inspector. Your passport please.'

He had the face of a whippet and the body language to match. He seemed to be in perpetual motion, ready to spring off in any direction. His hands moved with each word he uttered as if he was sculpting his own conversation in air.

Ezra handed him his passport. Cruz flipped through to the photograph and looked up at him, smiling.

'This is from long ago, yes?'

He handed the passport back and Ezra looked at his photo. The passport would be up for renewal in three months' time so the photo could not have been more than five years old. He was thinner then, thinner in the face. It had been taken during the dying years of his marriage.

'Come in my office, please.'

Ezra had expected to find an untidy desk piled high with papers and littered with coffee cups but Cruz's was immaculate. A large file folder with a Mont Blanc pen resting ostentatiously on top. A telephone, a jug of water, a glass, a small rubber plant and that was it.

The room was mercifully cool. An air-conditioning unit hummed in the corner window.

Cruz wiped the dust off a rubber plant with his handkerchief as he spoke.

'Why you come to Pinhão?'

'You asked to see me,' replied Ezra.

'No, no,' smiled the detective. 'My English. No good. Why you come here from Canada?'

'I'm writing a book about port.'

'You like port?'

'Yes.'

'They drink port in Canada?'

'They're beginning to.'

'Good. You write book, they drink more,' beamed Cruz.

'Could be.'

The detective stuffed his handkerchief into his breast pocket and picked up the letter opener that rested on an acrylic tray in his top drawer of his desk. He began to clean his nails.

'You have heard of Albino Lisboa Sousa?'

'Yes. He used to work for Mr Sykes.'

'Correct. When you last saw him?'

'Last night.'

Cruz opened the file in front of him with the tip of the letter knife.

'Ezra Brant,' he said, scanning a list of names. 'Yes. What time was it?'

'It must have been around midnight, maybe one o'clock.'

'Where you were?'

'I don't rightly know. That is, I don't know the name of the place. It was an abandoned farmhouse.'

'Senhor Brant. I know where were you. You are here on my list. I am not putting you in jail for spectating a fight with chickens. My jail will be full.'

'Well, that's a relief.'

'Then we understand me?'

Ezra nodded.

'Where you see him last?'

'I went outside during the cockfight

and I heard a police car siren so I went back in to warn . . . ah, the people there.'

'First, Senhora Katarina Soares.'

So Cruz knew they had been there together. He wondered what else Katarina had told the detective.

'That's right. We both left and that was the last time I saw him. May I ask what happened to him?'

'His, how you say . . . ' tapping his ribs with both hands.

'His lungs.'

'His lungs, yes. They are not full with water. He had a wound here.'

Cruz touched the left side of his forehead.

'And one more little something. His stomach. It had much port.'

'So you've done an autopsy? You pumped the stomach.'

The detective nodded.

'He was without his money. His bicycle was not there.'

'How do you explain that?' asked Ezra.

'Albino Sousa is wounded in front his head. The front, remember. He falls or maybe some person is pulling him into

227

the water. The question, how he is hurt on his head? And why there are no water in the lungs? Lungs, I learn a new English word. Thank you.'

'You're welcome.'

A drowning man would swallow water, Ezra thought, a corpse would not if it floated face-down.

'So you think it's murder,' he added, hoping Cruz might volunteer more information.

The phone rang and Cruz picked up the receiver, then put it down, shaking his head. He began drumming his fingers on the desk.

'Some person is phoning and only breathing. We will find him . . . Senhor Brant, you had argument with Albino Sousa before he is killed. What you were fighting?'

'It wasn't an argument. I was in the lagar treading grapes yesterday afternoon, no, it was evening. He came over to show me how I should clean off my legs. That's all. What time was this meant to have happened, anyway?'

If he could establish the time of Sousa's

death he might be able to use Katarina Soares as an alibi. Or maybe she could use him as her alibi.

Cruz turned another page in his file.

'Approximate two o'clock in the morning.'

The diminutive detective stood up and reached for a billiard cue that rested in the corner, then crossed to a map of the Douro on the wall. Three pins had been affixed at strategic points along the river. It amused Ezra to see the man standing in front of the map, tapping the point of the cue against it. Give a man a chart and a pointer and he begins to act like Field Marshal Montgomery.

'Here is you at the chicken fight. Here is the house of Albino Sousa. Here is place we find the body of Sousa.'

Ezra tried to estimate the distances. The spot on the river where the corpse had been found was roughly a mile and a half west of Quinta do Santo Pedro, just below Alvaro Soares' disputed vineyard where he had been shot at in the dovecot that morning. A dead body could have been carried downstream on the current but Sousa's house was almost due north of the abandoned quinta where the cockfight had taken place. Presumably he was on his way home when he met his fate. Cruz seemed to suggest that the wound to his forehead had been caused by a blow rather than a fall. And his bicycle had disappeared.

'How you know Senhora Katarina Soares?' the detective asked suddenly.

'I told you. I'm writing a book about port. In the course of my research I have to visit many quintas. Today I was at Quinta do Coteiro.'

'Today, yes. But yesterday you were with her.'

'We introduced ourselves at the railway station. I thought she had come to pick me up from the Oporto train and take me to Santo Pedro. I was told to look for a Mercedes, you see. And she happened to be there driving a Mercedes.'

Cruz nodded.

'But you were with her last night.'

'I went out for a walk about eleven o'clock. I couldn't sleep. She was driving by and stopped for me.'

'And she took you to the chicken fight.'

'Yes.'

Cruz made a check mark on a piece of paper and then leaned forward resting his chin on both his clenched hands. The left side of his jacket was vibrating, suggesting the agitated movement of his foot below the desk.

'Do you know this man?'

He whisked a photograph from the file and held it up close enough for Ezra to recognize the features of the American photographer he had been introduced to by Alvaro Soares.

'Yes, he's a professional photographer. His name is Ralph.'

'His name is Ralph Maddox. He is American.'

'What exactly is he doing here?' asked Ezra.

Cruz frowned and stood up to reassert his control of the interview.

'That is what I ask you.'

'All I know is what I was told. He's working on a new brochure for Alvaro Soares.'

'We are interested in Senhor Maddox.'

231

'Has he broken any of your laws?'

'He is known to us.'

Ezra knew that police the world over use this enigmatic phrase to imply that the person in question either has a criminal record or is under surveillance for the possible commission of a crime.

Cruz rose from his chair, perched on the edge of his desk and began swinging his leg.

'I imagine since you've got a photo of him that you've interviewed him.'

'Yes. You are correct. Before Portugal, he visited Libya.'

'I guess he will have travelled all over. Apparently he works for *National Geographic*.'

Cruz sat down at his desk again.

'Let us talk now about Luke Sykes. You know him, of course.'

'I met him yesterday for the first time. I've known his father for many years though.'

'He was with you last night, no?'

'You know he wasn't with me.'

Cruz smiled.

'Yes. I know he was not accompanied

with you. My question, where he was?'

'I imagine you've already asked him yourself,' said Ezra, irritated now by the man's circumlocutions which were even more tiresome when expressed in pidgin English.

'Yes. But I ask you.'

'I've no idea where he was.'

Cruz swung around in his seat to present Ezra with his profile. He stared at the ceiling tapping his fingertips together, a gesture he must have picked up from an American cop movie.

'How long you stay in Pinhão?'

'For three more days. I return to Canada on Monday.'

'It is my believe that Albino Sousa is murdered. I will find the man. You go now. You give me your passport.'

Ezra rose angrily from his chair to his full height.

'Are you telling me I'm a suspect and you're going to hold me here?'

'The investigation is not finished,' said Cruz.

'As far as I'm concerned,' said Ezra, 'this interrogation is finished.'

He turned and walked to the door, half expecting the little detective to spring from his seat and bar his way. Or to shout for back-up. But he could hear no movement behind him. He opened the door and kept walking, waiting for Cruz to call after him. But nothing was said.

It was dusk now and the plane trees that lined the street turned purple in the evening light. Ezra looked for Katarina Soares' Mercedes. He saw her standing smoking, looking in a shop window. As he approached she dropped the cigarette and ground it under her foot. She had draped a cardigan over her shoulders against the cool of the evening.

'I want to thank you for your discretion,' she said. 'My husband will find out I am here at the police station but I will tell him I needed my pills last night so I drove to the hospital.'

'And he'll believe you?'

She shrugged.

'He will pretend to believe me.'

'Did you know Albino Sousa?' asked Ezra.

'You sound like him in there,' replied

Katarina, indicating the police station with the merest movement of her head.

'Did you?'

'I don't know. I may have met him. It does not matter.'

'That detective, the little one, asked me if I knew the American photographer who's working for your husband.'

'Ralph. Yes, he asked me about him too. We are all suspects.'

'Has he interviewed your husband?'

'Why would he interview my husband?'

'You said we are all suspects.'

'This has nothing to do with Quinta do Coteiro. My husband was away. And he will be away again tomorrow so he can't attend the funeral. Besides the man was employed by your friend, Matthew Sykes, not my husband.'

There was a defensiveness in her manner that struck Ezra as strange. She had little sympathy for the victim and was distancing the murder from her husband and his enterprise.

'Was there anything about it in the local paper?' he asked.

'Maybe. I don't know. I don't read it.'

She had turned sullen and was no longer interested in their conversation.

'By the way. I still have your lighter and your cigarettes,' he said.

He reached into his pocket to get them but she had already begun to move away from him.

'I don't want them,' she said. 'You can keep them.'

★ ★ ★

Vasco was asleep in the driver's seat where Ezra had left him. He tapped the man on the shoulder through the open window and Vasco awoke with a jump. Ezra climbed into the passenger seat and waited for him to start the engine.

He thought about Cruz's map and the triangle of pins that marked the sites of the cockfight, Sousa's house and the point on the river where his body had been found. Something troubled him and he wasn't sure what it was. He needed a large-scale map that indicated the disposition of the vineyards, the road and its juxtaposition to the river. He conjured up in his mind Joseph Forrester's ten-foot-long map of the Douro framed in the Factory House. There was a reproduction of it in one of the pamphlets he had been sent by the Port Wine Institute when he had first embarked upon the research for his book. It would be ironic if Forrester's map could help him solve the mystery behind the death of Albino Sousa.

But perhaps there was a map at hand in the Mercedes' glove compartment. He opened it and shuffled through the papers there but it contained no maps.

'Do you have a map of the vineyards?' he asked Vasco. '*Mappa*.'

'Si, mappa,' nodded Vasco, and he pointed up to the hills in the direction they were heading. 'Quinta.'

Ezra would have to wait until they arrived back at the quinta.

'Tell me, Vasco. What do you think happened to Albino Sousa?'

The younger man drew his tongue nervously across his lips.

'Albino Sousa bad man.'

'Why bad?'

Vasco took one hand off the wheel and

moved his wrist as if he were flourishing a knife.

'He fought with a knife?'

'Many time.'

'Last night. Did he get into a fight last night?'

'Please?'

'Did he use his knife last night?'

'Please?'

Ezra gave up. He sat back in his seat looking out at the river that ran black now in the gathering darkness.

Vasco pulled the Mercedes up to where his truck was parked. He opened his door and ran around to the passenger side but Ezra was already out of his seat. He had to squeeze through the door since Vasco had not taken his girth into account when he parked so close to the truck.

On the front seat of the truck Ezra noticed a hessian sack. It looked just like the one Albino Sousa used to hold his fighting cock.

'Where did you get that?' he demanded, pointing at the sack.

Vasco regarded him with a vacant stare. The normally animated face became slack-jawed and the shoulders drooped.

'I said where did you get that?'

Ezra spoke slowly, enunciating every word, hoping that Vasco's comprehension of English would be enough to enable him to reply. Vasco stood in front of him, hanging his head, like a schoolboy knowing he was about to be punished. Ezra felt like shaking him.

'What's the matter?'

The voice was Luke's. He was standing by the entrance gate dressed in jeans and a denim shirt. He wore a New York Yankees ball cap.

Vasco let out a torrent of Portuguese. His tone was ingratiating and pleading at the same time.

'What's all this about a sack?' Luke asked Ezra.

'I just wondered where he got it, that's all.'

'Probably stole it,' said Luke, and then he addressed the question to Vasco in Portuguese.

'He says he found it down by the river. It was empty.'

Ezra opened the door to the truck and

reached over the seat for the hessian sack. There was a dark brown stain in the coarse burlap weave at the bottom. It looked like blood and powdered on his fingers when he rubbed it. He opened the sack and the smell reminded him of a henhouse.

'Ask him if there was a rooster in here when he found it?'

'What the dickens are you talking about?'

'Ask him, please.'

Luke put the question to Vasco who became animated once more.

'He swears it was empty. Now what the hell's going on?'

'Albino Sousa was carrying that sack last night.'

'What's all the commotion?' Matthew Sykes appeared through the gates.

'Damned if I know,' said Luke. 'You'd better tell him, Mr Brant.'

Ezra took a deep breath. The situation seemed to be getting out of hand.

'This sack was in Albino Sousa's possession last night. Vasco says he found it by the river. I'm just trying to establish where and when. It might have been the reason for his death.'

Sykes looked at Vasco who was clearly becoming more agitated by the minute. He leaned against his truck, hands deep in his pockets, staring up at the sky as if to invoke the intervention of his patron saint.

'How do you know it belonged to Albino Sousa?' asked Sykes.

'Because I saw him carrying it. He kept his rooster in it. I was at the cockfight last night.'

Father and son regarded him with incredulity.

'Cockfight? You went to a cockfight?'

Sykes looked angrily at Luke who held up his palms and shrugged.

'Don't look at me, Dad. I wasn't there.'

'Are you mad, Ezra? Do you realize what could have happened to you? What if the police had caught you there? And you did this as my guest, staying under my roof?'

'I'm sorry. It was a spontaneous thing. I didn't realize that I was abusing your hospitality. I thought it was local colour.'

241

Sykes barked at Vasco who scuttled into his truck and backed out down the track as if pursued by the hounds of hell.

The sound of the gong echoed across the courtyard beyond the walls.

'We waited dinner for you. I think we'd all better go in. I don't want to upset Gertrudes,' said Sykes, frostily. 'If you'll excuse me I have one call to make before I come to the table.'

★ ★ ★

A sheepish Ezra Brant knocked on Matthew Sykes' study door. Sykes was seated behind his desk and had just replaced the telephone in its cradle. On the blotting pad (Ezra had not seen one for years) was what appeared to be a legal document. Sykes removed it and slid it into the top drawer.

'I really must apologize,' said Ezra. 'I realize now I put you in a very compromising position. It was stupid of me.'

'Well, at least you got out before the police arrived,' said Sykes. 'Incidentally,

242

how did your interview go?'

'The cop wanted to keep my passport. He thinks I'm involved somehow. He asked me about Luke.'

'Luke?'

'Yes, he wanted to know his movements last night.'

'Is that all?'

'Yes.'

'And what did you tell him?'

'I have no idea where Luke was.'

Sykes frowned and looked away from Ezra to the bookshelves to his left. The lawyer's lamp on the desk with its green shade cast deep shadows across his face making him look old and worn out.

'What else did he ask?'

'He wanted to know if I knew an American photographer, Ralph Maddox. Does the name mean anything to you?'

Sykes shook his head.

'I'd like to know too,' said Ezra. 'There's an assignment guy on our photo desk in Toronto who's met everyone. Do you mind if I call him? I can charge it to my card.'

'By all means,' said Sykes, sliding the phone across the desk to him.

Ezra dialled the Canadian operator and asked to be connected to the *Toronto Examiner*'s news desk number.

The operator put the call through and Ezra asked to be transferred to the photo desk.

'Doc' Tattersall was a grizzled veteran of the Canadian newspaper business. He had emigrated to Canada in the 1970s from Fleet Street and he had brought with him that Rottweiler culture. A legendary insomniac, he preferred the graveyard shift since he avoided contact with managers young enough to be his children.

'Doc, hi! It's Ezra Brant. How are the Blue Jays doing?'

'Brant, now you didn't call me up from some god-forsaken foreign fleshpot to get the baseball scores. What's up?'

'I'm in the Douro Valley, port country.'

'I know where port comes from.'

'Listen, Doc. There's a photographer I need a lead on. He might be working for *National Geographic*. An American, named Ralph Maddox. Do you know him?'

'Ralph Maddox. Name's familiar. What's he use?'

'Nikon.'

'I knew a Maddox when I was in Australia, worked for the Murdoch chain. A paparazzo. A real brown-noser. What's he look like?'

'Mid-forties. Blond, close-cropped hair, blue eyes, medium build.'

'Sounds like him. Does he wear a fisherman's jacket? Lots of pockets?'

'Yes.'

'That's him. The freak.'

'Why do you say that?'

'The man's a snooper, a laundry sniffer. The only decent photo he ever took was Prince Charles looking at the Venus de Milo. Worldwide syndication on that one, otherwise he's strictly sleaze.'

'Thanks, Doc. I'll bring you back a bottle of port.'

'Vintage, Brant, none of your ruby crap.'

Ezra put the phone down. Why would Alvaro Soares hire an ambulance-chaser to shoot a brochure, he wondered? And how did he come to him in the first place?

Sykes had been sitting back staring out of the window during the conversation, lost in his own thoughts.

'What did he say?' asked Sykes.

'Ralph Maddox is an eavesdropper.'

'Oh,' said Sykes.

'Matthew,' said Ezra, 'Can I get hold of a map of the area? One that marks the vineyards?'

'You mean the Forrester map?'

'No, something contemporary.'

'Well, we do have one for this valley. In fact I had the surveyors make it for a legal action I'm involved in. I can lend you a copy.'

'That would be great.'

Sykes took out a bunch of keys from his waistcoat pocket and unlocked the bottom drawer of his desk. He rooted through the hanging files and pulled out a folded map.

'Let me have it back in the morning and I'll have it photostated for you, if you like.'

'Thank you.'

'Let's go in to dinner. I detest cold food.'

'Just one thing, Matthew.'

Ezra reached into his pocket and took out Amanda's wedding ring.

'I've been meaning to give this to you. I found it in the lagar when I was crushing.'

He handed the ring to Sykes who took it and inspected it under the lamp. He breathed heavily and nodded.

'You found it in the lagar?'

'Yes.'

'How extraordinary. It belongs to my wife,' he said. 'I imagine she will be pleased to have it back. Women put a lot of store by these things. Thank you. Shall we go in to dinner?'

Ezra had been hoping for an explanation as to how the ring came to be in the lagar but none was forthcoming and he did not press the issue.

On their way to the dining room, Sykes said, 'Tomorrow is Albino Sousa's funeral. I shall go, of course. Luke will too. Helen hasn't the time with all she has to do and there's no need for you to attend. But may I ask you a favour?'

'Certainly.'

'The guests will be arriving the day after tomorrow. Family members will expect to stay at the main house. So would you mind if we moved you into the guest house tomorrow?'

'Not at all.'

'Jolly good. Mmmm, that smells good. Gertrudes' cooking is the only thing that can get me out of a black mood.'

Just before they entered the dining room, Sykes put his hand on Ezra's sleeve to hold him back.

'I've decided to tell the police about the incidents,' he said. 'I think it's relevant now.'

★ ★ ★

The conversation at dinner had been self-consciously light. The three members of the Sykes family had made no mention of Albino Sousa's murder. They talked of the coming celebration and the publicity it would generate. Each of the guests would have the honour of putting their name to a young vine in the new vineyard and their name would be linked to it in perpetuity on a framed drawing showing its position in the row. Helen could not wait for the firework display and Luke confessed to his father that he had made a red table wine for the occasion — as a surprise — which he would like to have served at the dinner on the first night.

Matthew Sykes talked about the harvest and his anticipation of a great year. The mood at the table was buoyant and bantering.

Ezra sat listening to the animated conversation around him, wondering how each member of the family was dealing with the death of a man who had spent his life working at the quinta. For the first time since he arrived at Santo Pedro he was relieved to get up from the table and retire to his own room.

He spread the map Sykes had given him on the table under the light of the lamp and studied it. The scale was large enough to delineate the individual properties in the valley. Quinta do Santo Pedro and its vineyards had been shaded in red. Quinta do Coteiro in green. The vineyard where Sykes was having his marquee erected, with its six-month-old vines, was coloured with red stripes. It was situated to the right of the major vineyard, rising to Soares' acreage where he had been shot at in the dovecot. About a half-mile to the left was a hexagonal-shaped vineyard that had been marked with similar red stripes. It fell away to the road which ran very close to the river at this point.

Ezra pictured in his mind's eye the map that Cruz had shown him. The point where they had found the body was at a bend in the river. The bend appeared to be directly below Quinta do Coteiro. Vasco Gedes had found the hessian sack by the river. Could the vineyard manager have been Albino Soares' assailant? He could have come across Soares pedalling his bicycle while he himself was driving home. He had an old score to settle perhaps . . .

But the police were on that road. Vasco would have heard the siren as they all had. If he had intended harm to Sousa that would not have been the time to take his revenge. Ezra tried to find the place where the police car had stopped the truck but it could have been anywhere along a two-mile stretch of road.

Yet something still did not make sense. Albino Sousa would have headed home at that hour. The village of Cotas was north of the pin the detective had used to mark the ruined quinta where the cockfight had taken place. His body had been found a good mile and a half east in the direction of the quintas of Santo Pedro and Coteiro. Soares would not want to be caught by the police cycling home carrying a sack containing a fighting cock, he reasoned. He must have given the sack to someone who was in a better position than he to ensure that it would not be found by the police.

He must have given it for safe-keeping to Vasco Gedes. Yet Vasco swore he had found the sack and it had been empty. He swore, according to Luke, but he didn't swear on his mother's grave as someone in his position would have done if he really wanted to express his innocence. Supposing Vasco was keeping the cock for

Soares and he hears that Soares is dead. What would his instincts have told him? To keep the bird until someone asked him for it. But why carry the sack around in his truck?

★ ★ ★

Ezra awoke late the next morning. He had missed Anna Figueira's knock on the door because the cup of tea she had left outside it was stone cold. The milk had congealed in a white circle on top.

His breakfast place had been set at the dining table but there was no sign that Sykes or his son had eaten. He sat down and rang the bell on the table expecting Anna or her aunt Maria to respond to it. Instead, Helen entered with a glass of fresh orange juice.

'You must have slept well last night,' she said. 'No snakes.'

'No snakes. Matthew and Luke are out and about already, are they?'

'Yes, they're pall-bearers. They have to get the coffin from the house and carry it to the graveyard. They do it early before the heat of the day.'

'Tell me, Helen, did Albino Sousa ever come to this house?'

'Of course, he was Matthew's farm manager. He was always here discussing the running of the quinta. When to spray, how radically to prune, which block to pick first, when to truck the wine to Vila Nova de Gaia. What would you like for breakfast? Eggs and bacon?'

'Eggs and bacon would be fine. Was he in the house in the last couple of days?'

'I don't know. He may have been, to speak with Luke while Matthew was away. At harvest time there's a lot of decisions to be made.'

'How did he get on with Vasco Gedes?'

'Vasco? Everybody gets on with Vasco. He's always smiling. And you should see him dance. I think he's sweet on Maria. He's forever hanging around the kitchen.'

'I met Albino Sousa's brother. Luis.'

'Poor chap.'

'What exactly happened to him?'

'The story I heard was that Luis was working the tractor alone in the new vineyard. It must have been May, no,

June. They had been dynamiting in the morning, breaking up the rocks. His tractor tipped over and he hit his head. He was pinned under it for several hours until Albino found him. Matthew called Alvaro Soares and asked him if he could fly Luis to the hospital in Oporto in his helicopter. It would take too long for the ambulance to get here. But it was too late anyway. His brain had already been damaged and he had spent too long lying in the sun. Matthew still pays him a weekly wage.'

Ezra ate his eggs and bacon in solitude and thought about Albino Sousa. He had attacked Luke with a knife when the young man had refused to marry his pregnant daughter. And then his only brother had been reduced to a dancing cretin by an accident that had occurred on Sykes' land. Had Sousa blamed the Sykes family for that too? Was he behind the incidents that kept occurring at Quinta do Santo Pedro? If so, what did Soares have to gain by the misfortunes that dogged Matthew Sykes?

In the distance Ezra could hear the

noise of a helicopter taking off. Alvaro Soares was leaving Quinta do Coteiro as Katarina said he would. Soares had agreed to help fly the wounded Luis to hospital in Oporto. It was interesting that warring neighbours could drop their feud to perform a humanitarian act. Perhaps Katarina could enlighten him further about the whole incident.

The jeep, Sykes had told him, was at his disposal. He drove out of the quinta and down to the road that would lead him up to Soares' property.

He parked next to Ralph Maddox's blue truck and looked around for its mysterious owner. There was no one about so he decided to take a look inside. He tried the back doors. They were unlocked so he let himself in.

The interior of the truck was illuminated by an eerie amber light. It had been set up as a mobile darkroom. Along the driver's side was a stainless steel workbench with a sink and water cistern mounted above it. Plastic containers of developing fluid, fixative and Permawash were set into a shelf above the counter. A

Leica Focomat enlarger stood at the far end next to a light box and a paper safe. Snaky lengths of processed negatives hung inside a transparent acrylic chest behind the enlarger.

A bunch of black and white photos had been strung by clips along a line to dry. He looked closely at them. There were candid shots of harvesters in the vineyard and flatbeds carrying hods of grapes. Close-ups of Alvaro Soares and Katarina wearing her perennial headscarf.

And then he caught sight of himself. There were photos of him entering the dovecot with Matthew Sykes in the background.

His heart began to beat more quickly.

There were other shots of him too. In Oporto near the *rabelos* with Sykes as they walked along the quay. And next to these hung a grainy photo of Luke with his arms around a woman. The shot had been taken at night. Luke was kissing her. His head obscured hers but Ezra could tell from the hairstyle that the woman was Helen Sykes.

There was another photo of Luke and

Helen walking through a vineyard at night.

At the end of the line were two shots of a woman in her late fifties wearing a large white hat. She was holding the hat to her head against the wind. On her finger was a wedding ring. Amanda Sykes. She was accompanied by a younger man in a business suit.

All the shots appeared to have been taken with a long telephoto lens.

Why was Maddox documenting the goings-on at Quinta do Santo Pedro? Since Alvaro Soares had hired him it must have been on the owner's instructions.

Ezra's speculations were interrupted by a sudden burst of light as the truck door opened.

'What the hell are you doing in here?'

Ralph Maddox stood menacingly in the entrance, crouching slightly as if he was about to spring at Ezra. In his hand, instead of the habitual camera, was a Browning semi-automatic pistol, the kind issued to American Army officers.

Ezra thought fast.

'I was waiting for you.'

'You didn't have to break into my truck.'

'Sorry, I thought you might be inside. Do you mind putting that gun down.'

Maddox lowered the weapon.

'Outside,' he said.

Maddox backed out, never taking his eyes off Ezra.

After the dim ochre light of the truck the sunshine was blinding. Ezra waited for Maddox to speak.

'Okay, so what were you looking for?'

'I told you. I was looking for you. I need some illustrations for the article I'm writing. I thought we could do some business.'

'Yeah? What do you pay for one use?'

'$250 a shot. Canadian, that is.'

'Chicken feed.'

Maddox slipped the revolver into his belt.

'I start at $1,000. US.'

'I see you've got shots of me. Very flattering.'

Maddox shrugged.

'I'm a shooter. I'm into portraits. Might

do a coffee table book. *Faces Observed*, I'll call it.'

'Using a long lens?'

'You get the real person with telephoto. The camera lies, my friend, because it makes the subject lie.'

Ezra had the feeling that he had used the line before and that it was not his in the first place.

'What are you going to do with those photos of the Sykes family?'

Maddox squinted off into the distance, measuring his response.

'Sykes family?'

'Those people down there,' said Ezra, and as soon as he uttered the words he understood what was going on.

Soares had hired Maddox, a paparazzo who was good at his sleazy trade, to provide documentary evidence of the Sykes' incursions into vineyard land he claimed to be his. But Maddox had gone beyond his brief and had shot more than his employer had asked him to. He had captured an affair between Luke and Helen on film. That hand-in-hand walk in the vineyard at night was obviously on the same roll as the shots of himself by the quay in Oporto and those of him entering the dovecot.

The photos raised more questions than they answered. Did Maddox catch Luke and Helen on their way to the guest cottage the night Albino Sousa was murdered? And who was the man with Amanda Sykes?

'Just candid stuff, messing around,' replied Maddox. 'Anyway, I gotta go. I'm shooting a funeral. Should get some interesting stuff.'

'Tell me, how did you meet Mr Soares?'

Maddox was walking towards the driver's door. He stopped and turned.

'He and his wife were vacationing on a Greek island owned by some Hong Kong tycoon. I was snorkelling, taking photos of some minor royal bathing topless. He swam up beside me. We got talking and he invited me here. End of story.'

'And Libya?'

'Libya! How the hell did you know about Libya?'

'The cop in Pinhão. He interviewed you.'

Maddox whistled.

'Boy, word travels fast around here. I'd had a tip-off that Ghaddafi was going to give a big money prize to a black guy, an Islamic fundamentalist from New York. A humanitarian award he called it, for several million bucks. I could have sold that photo around the world.'

'What happened?'

'I got stopped at the border and held in their fucking jails for three days because I had a case of Jack Daniels in my truck. They thought I was trying to sell it.'

A woman's voice cut into their conversation.

'Jack Daniels stays on your breath. I drink vodka.'

The two men turned to see Katarina Soares leaning against a pillar, a glass dangling from her fingers. She wore tailored white trousers and a floral silk blouse. Her feet were bare and her scalp was covered by a close-fitting white turban with a large emerald brooch pinned to the front.

'Ezra, how nice of you to come to keep me company just as Ralph is leaving,' she said.

Maddox grinned and opened the door of his truck. Ezra moved towards the house.

'If you can raise your price to $500 we might do business,' Maddox called to Ezra.

'Too steep for our rag.'

'Your loss.'

'Guess so,' responded Ezra, as he watched Maddox reverse and make a three-point turn.

'Will you join me?' said Katarina, holding her lipstick-stained glass aloft and jiggling the ice at him.

'Too early in the day for me but I'll have some mineral water,' replied Ezra.

He followed her inside. A maid was hoovering the Persian carpet that expanded in glowing reds and blues across the entrance hall. Katarina nearly tripped over the wire. She giggled at the maid's expression of consternation.

'You're in a good mood today,' said Ezra.

'Of course. Alvaro is taking me on a cruise to Hawaii as soon as the crush is finished.'

She made her way over to the drinks cabinet in the living room and reached for the vodka bottle.

'Don't you love the name, Smirnoff? It sounds like a Russian swear word. Smirnoff. Smirnoff.'

She grimaced theatrically as she repeated the name.

'Did you say mineral water, Ezra?'

'Yes, please.'

She grabbed a fistful of ice from the container and dropped it into a glass. She splashed a bottle of mineral water into it until it overflowed.

'Oops. The glass is too small. Don't look at me with such disapproval, Ezra.'

'It's not disapproval. I was only thinking that alcohol isn't the answer.'

'It is when you don't know the question.'

'May I ask you a very personal one?'

She handed him the glass of mineral water which was still dripping.

'I may not answer but go ahead.'

'You told me the other night that you're dying of cancer. How long have the doctors given you?'

'Doctors! What do they know? I know in here.'

Her eyes were flashing. She stood above him patting her left breast.

'And what is *your* prognosis, Dr Katarina?'

'That I will live till I die . . . I mean *really* live.'

She sat on the arm of Ezra's chair and ran her fingers through his hair. Her fingers were cool and he felt a surge of excitement in his stomach.

'You have lovely hair, so white and thick.'

To distract her he said, 'I would have thought you'd be at the funeral this morning.'

'I have no interest in other people's deaths. The only funeral I will attend will be my own. And maybe not even that one.'

She took a gulp from her glass.

Ezra realized that every reference to death made her drink more heavily. He felt a wave of pity mingled with a jabbing sense of shame. He was torn between his attraction to this beautiful, doomed woman and his need to extract information from her.

She was curling his hair around her index finger. He could smell the peach-like fragrance of her skin and feel the warmth of her breast on his shoulder as she leant over him. He had a sudden desire to pull her down to him and bury his face in the whiteness of her neck. The maid had disappeared and they were alone now. She was crying out to him to show her that she had life in her still but something was holding him back. A misplaced sense of chivalry or perhaps her explicit signals unnerved him.

'Katarina, do you remember Albino Sousa ever coming here?'

'Here to the house?'

'Yes.'

'Once I saw him.'

'When was that?'

'Early in the summer. His brother Luis had been badly injured. A tractor fell on him. I remember because I took the telephone call. Mr Sykes told me. He asked Alvaro for the helicopter to take him to hospital.'

'Did your husband fly with Luis Sousa to the hospital?'

'No, there is only two seats. Alvaro's pilot and Luis. Why do you ask so many questions?'

Ezra ignored her remark.

'Did Albino Sousa talk to your husband?'

'Of course. He was here many hours, waiting for news of his brother. Now enough of the questions. If you will not drink with me then you will have to make love to me. And if you say it is too early in the day for you I will shoot you.'

She pointed two fingers at him, cocked her thumb and made the sound of a shot.

'And if I asked for vodka?' said Ezra, smiling.

'I would pour it over your head,' she said, laughing.

'I'm sure you would,' said Ezra.

He put a hand on her cheek and kissed her gently on the lips.

'Come,' she said, taking him by the

hand. 'Don't worry about the maid. She is deaf.'

Katarina led him down the hall. She opened a door to a bedroom furnished with a four-poster bed trimmed with lace. Apart from the polished oak of the bed, everything in the room was white, even to the pot of wild rock roses on the bedside table. The only incongruous note was the presence of a small teddy bear nestling between the pillows. Its head was covered with a silk handkerchief in ironic imitation of its owner's.

Ezra heard Katarina lock the door behind them. When he turned around she was naked to the waist and her eyes were closed as if she were listening to some celestial music of her own.

★ ★ ★

She fed him slices of pineapple marinated in orange juice that dripped all over the sheets. They laughed and showered and it was only when they had dressed that Katarina became withdrawn.

For his part Ezra had never felt so

young. Their lovemaking had been passionate and intense, a coupling of two people trying to plumb the depths of their individual needs.

It had been some time since Ezra had made love. The woman he was seeing in Toronto, a divorcee like himself but without children, was an international labour lawyer who spent much of her life on aeroplanes flying between the world's capitals. His own travel meant they connected once, maybe twice a month. He did not feel he was being unfaithful to her since there was no commitment on either side. Shauna Mulligan, as Irish as her name, black Irish in this case, enjoyed her freedom too much to move in with him. She expected no more than to be taken to dinner, a concert or a movie and then to bed to enjoy each other in comfort. She got on well with Michael although Ezra had tried to keep them apart at first, fearful that his son might like her too much (a surrogate mother) or not at all.

But making love to Katarina, her bald head sprouting the suggestion of a blond fuzz, had been exciting and he felt a reeling dizziness from the experience as if it had been his first time.

'What is it like to make love to a dying woman?' she had asked him as she refreshed her drink.

'How can you be dying when you have so much to give?' he replied.

'It's true,' she said, handing him the single malt he had asked for. Macallan eighteen-year-old, the perfect post-coital whisky.

'There's something I'd like to do,' he said. 'Your husband mentioned that the Baron de Forrester may have stayed here. He said his family kept the guest books going back to that period. Would it be possible for me to see them?'

'They're not here,' said Katarina. 'They were just gathering dust in the library so he sent them to the Institute in Oporto. Alvaro has a memory like a sieve.'

Ezra's face registered his disappointment.

'This might sound ghoulish but I'd like to see the spot where he drowned. I dreamed about it a few days ago. It was like an out-of-body experience. I want to see if it looks the way it did in my dream. Will you come?'

'Where is it?'

'The Valeira dam. I need to see it for my book.'

'There is a shrine in the hills above it. A hermitage in the rock of San Salvador do Mundo,' she said. 'I will show you the way.'

As they walked to the jeep Katarina told him to wait for a moment. She hurried back inside the house and returned a few moments later with a torch.

'What's that for?' he asked.

'It's a surprise. It will be my gift to you.'

She refused to tell him more, smiling enigmatically at his questions.

They drove down the rutted track to the main road and through the town of Pinhão.

'Take the bridge to the other side of the river and follow the signs to San Joao da Pesqueira,' she said. 'This way we can avoid Cotas and the funeral procession.'

They worked their way up the snaking road through the town of Ervedosa do Douro and up to the treeline. To their right the mighty swells of granite rock rose to a cloudless blue sky.

'Keep going,' she said, as they approached San Joao da Pesqueira.

There was something urgent in her tone as if their drive together had become a mission.

'We're going there,' she said, pointing to a chapel perched on top of a mountain peak. 'San Salvador do Mundo.'

The wind blew in their faces, bringing tears to their eyes, as they looked down on the massive concrete dam that arced like a bow across the river. A road had been built above it and behind it the river funnelled to its narrowest point. That must have been the point where the gorge was before it was dynamited to widen he river, thought Ezra. The place where Joseph Forrester had met his fate. He wished he had flowers, red roses, to cast into the water as a tribute to the Baron.

Katarina must have read his thoughts.

'Throw some money in the water. For

good luck,' she said.

He took out the loose change in his pocket and flung it as far as he could. He tried to follow its flight but he could not for the tears in his eyes. Genuine tears not caused by the wind. Nor could he hear the sound of the coins striking the water for the rumble of the wind.

Ezra looked down at the still, deep water. In his dream he had seen the furious turbulence of the rapids as the water roared through the gorge. The lake created by the dam was as still as a millpond but the rocky slopes on which he stood in his dream were the same and in the cry of the birds that circled on the air currents above him he could hear the screams of the drowning. Joseph Forrester, weighed down by the gold in his money belt and high boots full of the Douro that he loved, had vanished in these waters. The river had become his grave.

He wondered how Forrester's children had taken the news of their father's death. He had fathered seven children in all: James, Joseph James, Ermelinda whom the family called Emmie, Eliza, William Offley (named after his godfather, Forrester's partner), Frank Woodhouse (named for his friend and fellow port shipper, Robert Woodhouse) and the baby Maria, who had died with her mother during Oporto's typhoid epidemic in 1847. A nurse who visited the house infected Eliza Forrester and her newborn baby with the disease. Mother and daughter were buried in the cemetery of the British Church in Oporto and Forrester was forced to send his six young children back to England to be cared for by relatives and friends. Reminiscent of his own childhood, thought Ezra. When his mother had died, his father, a doctor, had sent him to boarding school and even on school holidays he saw little of him.

Katarina's voice broke into his thoughts.

'This is my favourite place in the Douro,' she said.

'It's beautiful,' said Ezra, and he put his arm around her shoulders.

'In Forrester's day that would have been a gorge down there and there would have been rapids just about at that point where the river narrows.'

'When was he drowned?'

'May 12th, 1861. It was a Sunday.'

'May 12th,' she said. 'Two days after my anniversary . . . Will you always remember me Ezra?'

'How can I forget you, Katarina?'

'Men forget . . . I feel I want to tell you something. About my life that I cannot tell my husband. I know I have little time left and there are things I would rather not confess to a priest. What do they know of life, let alone death? If I told you here in this beautiful place surely God would listen and forgive me.'

'I think He would.'

She moved away from him and sat down on the wind-smoothed rock of the mountain, her arms locked around her knees.

'I love my husband and I was faithful to him all the time I have been married to him. Except when I found out I had leukaemia. I was so frightened. I told no one for many weeks, not even my

274

husband. And I took a lover. I wanted so desperately to cling to life. One day after we had made love I told him. That was the last time I looked into his eyes. The only word he heard was 'cancer'. He got scared. He told me to go to my husband and that was the end between us.'

'I'm sorry,' said Ezra. 'That was a rotten thing for him to do.'

'You know who I am talking about, don't you.'

'I think I do,' said Ezra.

Katarina Soares stood up and smiled wearily.

'It was Luke Sykes, wasn't it?'

She said nothing and turned her head away so that he would not see her cry.

Ezra felt a pang of jealousy. Luke, the careless Lothario, causing misery with each conquest. Even his father seemed exasperated by his endless need to seduce every woman who crossed his path. What were the words Matthew had used when Albino Sousa took his revenge with a knife? 'A little blood-letting satisfied honour all round.' He had thought Matthew callous when he had said it but knowing now of Luke's involvement with Katarina and Helen, he would have wished for a harsher punishment than a scarred thumb.

Yet how had Luke reacted to Albino Sousa going for him with a knife? Did he accept the cut as the end of the matter or did he harbour his own thoughts of revenge? Seeing them together in the lagar they appeared to have made their peace with each other. In spite of his attack on Luke, Sousa remained in the company's employ and Luke was still on speaking terms with him. But Luke's whereabouts on the night of the farm manager's murder were not accounted for. Unless he was with Helen in the guest house.

'Did Luke like watching the cock-fights?'

'Why do you ask?'

Katarina's voice was harsh.

'Just curious.'

'Are you crazy? Do you think we would risk being seen together? My husband would have killed him. If he had not killed me first.'

She laughed, a mirthless laugh.

'It's funny really when you think about it. Alvaro is suing your friend Mr Sykes and I am sleeping with his son. Was sleeping with his son. Past tense, right?'

'How do you think it will end?'

'Alvaro is a proud man. He is used to winning. He has lots of money and he knows Quinta do Santo Pedro is mortgaged, how do you say? To the hilt. The legal fees are bleeding Mr Sykes. He will have to give up the land.'

'How do you feel about that?'

Katarina picked up a pebble and rolled it down the slope of the rock like a marble. She watched it bounce until it disappeared from view.

'I understand why Alvaro wants the land. It belonged to his family many, many years ago. But for me, it doesn't matter. I have no future.'

Katarina's mood swings disconcerted Ezra. From moment to moment he could not gauge her reaction to him or to his questions. But he was determined to pump her for information that might help him understand why Albino Sousa had ended up in the Douro with his head bashed in.

'You must have met Amanda Sykes.'

'Yes. Like all the English women here she wore ridiculous hats. And her shoes! I think there must be a special store for prison warders in England where she bought them.'

'I've never met her. She lives in Lisbon, apparently.'

He tried to disguise his interest in the vagueness of his reply.

'Her cook Gertrudes is a cousin to my gardener so I hear a lot of things.'

'What sort of things?'

'You men. You like gossip as much as women.'

She moved the fingers of both hands like the tentacles of an octopus.

'You're probably right.'

'Did you know Mrs Sykes is suing her husband for divorce?'

'On what grounds?'

'Adultery.'

'You're kidding! Matthew Sykes? Who's the woman?'

'Oh come now. Haven't you got eyes in your head?'

'I've hardly seen him.'

'His niece, Helen.'

'But — '

Ezra caught himself before he could give voice to his surprise. Surely she must mean that Luke is having an affair with Helen. He did not want to spring this information on Katarina in case she was unaware of it. From what she had told him she had been hurt enough by Luke. But as he reflected on this revelation matters began to become clearer. Helen's tears, her sadness and her general demeanour were consistent with the behaviour of a woman who had been confused and torn emotionally by the amorous attentions of a father and son.

Helen had always referred to Sykes as a relative she was grateful to and not as a lover. But that was obviously only for my benefit, he realized. Or maybe for Luke's as well. Did he know of his father's involvement with Helen? Did Matthew know of Luke's?

If Matthew Sykes had been having an

affair with his niece and Amanda had got wind of it no wonder she never wanted to set foot in Quinta do Santo Pedro again. That would also explain the presence of the wedding ring in the lagar. In a fit of anger Amanda must have pulled it from her finger and thrown it at her husband. But Matthew had not been at the quinta the night that Amanda had stayed there. According to Helen, he had been in Oporto, sleeping at his club. Amanda's confrontation must have been with someone else. Her niece Helen, perhaps.

'There is too much going on in that head of yours,' said Katarina. 'Come, it's time I gave you your surprise.'

She took him by the hand and led him back to the jeep.

'Where are we going?' he asked.

'You'll see. Let me drive.'

He tossed her the keys, opened the door for her and got into the passenger seat.

The drive down to the river was the most terrifying experience Ezra had ever had in a car. Even the drivers of Cairo who have one foot permanently on the accelerator, the other on the horn, were no match for Katarina Soares. He gripped the dashboard with both hands as she threw the jeep around the hairpin turns, skidding off the gravel surface of the uneven road. Katarina shrieked with delight at every slide and sideways movement of the vehicle.

'Take it easy,' shouted Ezra. 'You're going to kill us both.'

He was sweating when they reached the main road that would take them down through Ervedosa to the Rio Torto, one of the many tributaries of the mighty Douro.

'That's Bom Retiro up there,' said Katarina, pointing to a quinta set above a magnificent sweep of vineyards. 'They make a lovely twenty-year-old tawny. They're owned by Ramos-Pinto, the company with the sexy posters. The founder Adriano Ramos-Pinto liked women so much he had them imported from Paris. That was over one hundred years ago.'

After crossing the bridge into Pinhão she turned left along the river, past

Calem, in the direction of her husband's quinta.

Ezra thought he recognized the road that led off the highway to the abandoned farmhouse where he had witnessed his first cockfight.

'Okay,' he said, 'I give up. Where are you taking me?'

'Not far,' she replied. 'But you must promise me one thing.'

'What's that?'

'What I am going to show you only my husband has seen. It is a secret and you must tell no one. Do you promise?'

'I promise.'

She was silent for the rest of the drive.

Ezra's curiosity was mounting with every twist in the road. They were approaching Sykes' new vineyard and the bend in the river where Albino Sousa's body had been found.

Katarina pulled the jeep off the road and stopped.

'Bring the torch,' she said. 'This is my gift to you. It is our secret just as our lovemaking is our secret. You promised me.'

'Our secret,' he repeated, handing her the torch.

She moved towards the river where the rocky bank fell away steeply into the water. He followed her across the granite boulders, his arms extended to help him balance. She disappeared from his view as he manoeuvred his way down through the broken rocks to the water's edge.

'Katarina,' he called.

'Over here.'

She was standing in a cleft of rock next to a dead ilex bush. His eyes were riveted to the rocks under his feet as he picked his way over to where she stood. The surface was slippery and he was fearful of falling.

'Come this way.'

The cleft in the rock where she stood seemed to face a granite wall. She disappeared for an instant.

'Where are you?'

'I'm here,' she said, reappearing. 'It's hard to find the entrance. It's like a code. You have to know the rocks.'

He moved towards her and took her outstretched hand. She pulled him to her.

'Remember your promise,' she said, kissing him lightly on the lips. 'Now, keep holding my hand and shut your eyes. Don't open them until I tell you to. I will guide you.'

He closed his eyes and he heard the click of the torch. She pulled him gently forward.

'It's very narrow here,' she said. 'You'll have to move sideways. But keep your eyes shut and trust me.'

He could feel the coolness of the rock as his back scraped against it. His eyelids registered the growing darkness as he moved forward. And then the smell hit him. A stench of rotting vegetation and dampness. His footsteps began to echo. They were in some kind of cave.

There was a flapping sound and Katarina screamed. He opened his eyes and could only see the beam of light trained on the floor.

'Katarina! Are you all right?'

'It was just a bat. It gave me a fright, that's all . . . Now. Look over here.'

She flashed the torch on the wall of the cave and began to move it slowly across the face of the rock.

The circle of light illuminated drawings of animals in black, yellow and ochre. They seemed to be in flight, moving deeper into the cave, as if fleeing an unseen hunting party whose scent they had picked up on the wind. Horned deer-like creatures with graceful legs, wild boar as large as buffalo with curling tusks and a bear-like creature rearing up on its back legs.

'This is absolutely amazing!' exclaimed Ezra.

'Isn't it beautiful?' said Katarina.

Ezra approached the wall and ran his fingers lightly over the shapes. He had seen the Lascaux caves in Burgundy and the style of the drawings appeared to be very similar. Those palaeolithic rock carvings were a national treasure that attracted tourists from all over the world.

'How did you find this?' asked Ezra.

'Alvaro found it.'

'It's magnificent. Look at those colours. They're so fresh and bright but they must be thousands of years old. How far does it go?'

'I'm not sure,' said Katarina. 'Let's find out.'

They worked their way deeper into the cave, the torch pointed at the ground, flicking occasionally to the wall to discover more drawings.

'Imagine,' said Katarina, 'an artist so long ago working down here by the light of a fire, with a burnt stick and colours made from plants.'

The animals on the wall seemed to be alive. Ezra could almost hear their breathing as they galloped across the granite wall. He felt a sudden exhilaration, a sense of wellbeing as if he had been connected to a primordial past through the sinewy charcoal lines that had brought these animals to life.

'You can't keep this a secret forever,' he said.

'Alvaro will do what he has to do,' she replied. 'Meanwhile we cover the entrance with a bush so no one can find it.'

Ezra felt a downdraught that made him shiver. The air was fresher here. He could hear a distant rumbling that grew in volume and then faded away again. It sounded like a car.

We must be under the road, he thought.

'I don't know how much further it goes,' said Katarina, shining the torch on a pile of rock. 'I'm getting cold. I want to go back.'

The gust of air was stronger here and Ezra, whose eyes had become accustomed to the darkness, looked up to find its source. Directly above the rock pile was a crevice in the ceiling. Through the pencil-thin crack he could see the sky.

'Ezra, please come. I'm getting cold.'

He returned to her side and they began to move towards the mouth of the cave.

'It makes me want to cry,' said Katarina. 'There are so many beautiful things in the world that I have not seen.'

Ezra put his arm around her shoulder. He could feel her bare skin stippled with gooseflesh. All at once she cried out and dropped the torch. She collapsed to her knees.

'Ow! My toe. I stubbed my toe.'

'Don't move.'

Ezra knelt down, picked up the torch

and shone it on her foot.

'Can you walk?'

'I think so.'

He put the torch down, pointing in the direction they were moving and helped her to her feet. When he went to retrieve the torch his eye was caught by something shining on the rocky floor. It was a tiny loop of gold. Like a link from a chain that had broken. He wetted his finger and pressed it against the link, placing it carefully in his shirt pocket.

'Let me lean on you,' she said, as they walked slowly towards the entrance.

As they moved Ezra silently counted his paces.

Once outside in the sunshine again Katarina replaced the dead bush over the opening and looked around to see if there was anyone in sight.

'Our secret, remember,' she said, placing a finger on his lips.

* * *

She had kissed him goodbye at the entrance to her husband's quinta. She asked him to drop her there, suggesting that it would be best if he left now. Perplexed by her mercurial change of mood he said nothing.

She had him promise again that he would tell no one what he had seen. He affirmed his silence once more and watched her walk slowly away up the driveway. She had turned, smiled at him and then continued walking.

On the drive back down to Quinta do Santo Pedro he thought about the cave and an idea started to form in his mind.

As soon as he had parked the jeep, he made straight for his room and unfolded the map that Matthew Sykes had lent him. He located where he thought the cave was situated, moving his finger inland from a point on the river. The cave had run under the main road. He looked at the scale of the map and tried to convert the forty-three paces he had counted off into a linear measure. Given that distance, if he and Katarina had been under the road then they would have to have been at a point where the road ran closest to the Douro.

The only point where this happened was just below Sykes' vineyard where Luis Sousa had suffered his terrible accident.

Ezra thought about the rush of air and the sight of the sky through the roof of the cave.

There must have been another way in. And that way in was from Sykes' vineyard.

The more he thought about it the more convinced he became that Albino Sousa had been murdered. He now knew the reason. He would need to ask more questions to find out who was the killer.

★   ★   ★

Ezra showered and put on a clean shirt. He hummed to himself as he brushed his hair. It was a song he heard his father sing while he shaved. An Ivor Novello song, was it?

We'll gather lilacs in the Spring again,
I'll take you down a shady lane,

And in the evening by the firelight's
  glow
I'll hold you tight and never let you
go.'

Ezra had vowed he would never sing in
the shower or as he shaved. He hated
hearing his father warbling in the
mornings. But now Ezra found himself
emulating him. He wondered if Michael
found his bathroom tenor as offensive as
he had found his own father's.

He glanced at his watch. It was six
o'clock, the usual time for drinks in the
courtyard. But no table had been set up.

He wandered to the iron gate and
looked down the valley to see if Matthew
Sykes' Mercedes was anywhere in sight
but there was no vehicle on the road.

He remembered that Sykes had
requested that he move into the guest
house and he wondered if it had been set
up for him. He decided to stroll down to
take a look in order to pass the time
before Matthew and Luke Sykes returned
from the funeral or wherever they were.

Helen Sykes let out a startled shriek when he opened the door to the guest house.

'You gave me such a fright,' she said.

She had been bending over the bed, making hospital corners with the blankets.

'I'm sorry. I wasn't sure when Matthew wanted me to move down here.'

'Don't worry,' said Helen. 'We'll have Vasco bring your case down. He can pack for you if you like.'

'That's all right. I'll do it myself. I have a thing about packing.'

He wondered how he might broach the subject of Amanda Sykes in the light of what Katarina had told him. He stood watching her waiting for her to speak.

'There's an electric heater in the closet in case you feel cold at night,' she said, fussing with the bed to keep her hands busy. 'It can get a little damp being so close to the river.'

'Helen, may I ask you something?'

She turned towards him and he could see the blood rising in her cheeks.

'Isn't it silly. I always blush when people say things like that to me.'

Her hands moved to her throat as if their touch would dissipate the high colour in her cheeks.

'Your uncle invited me here because he wanted me to find out who was behind all those weird incidents that kept happening. Did he tell you?'

Helen nodded, fearful of what was to follow.

'I think I know now who's behind them but I want to be sure before I tell your uncle. So can I ask you a few questions?'

'Do you mind if I sit down?'

'Please.'

She crossed to the table, as far away from the bed as she could get, and pulled out a chair.

'Something happened here the night before I arrived. I think it involved Amanda Sykes,' Ezra began.

'Why do you say that?'

'Because of the ring I found in the lagar. She threw it there, didn't she? Or more likely she threw it at someone and it ended up in there.'

Helen clutched the seat of the chair and looked despairingly at the door.

'It's okay. Whatever you tell me will remain strictly between us. What I don't understand is why Amanda would stay over at the quinta if she had vowed never to set foot in the place again?'

Helen let out a contemptuous laugh.

'Because she's too stingy to book a hotel room if you really want the truth.'

'She came here with a man, didn't she?'

Helen nodded.

'Do you know who he was?'

'He was a lawyer, Desmond Grenville-Smith. He works for an English law firm in Oporto.'

'Did they sleep in the same room?'

Helen threw back her head and laughed.

'Are you thinking she was having an affair with a younger man?'

'I don't know,' replied Ezra. 'I'm just trying to fit things together.'

'No. They had separate bedrooms. That wasn't Auntie Amanda's style. In fact I don't think she's very interested in that sort of thing.'

'But her husband is.'

Helen looked fiercely at him.

'And just what do you mean by that!'

'You know what I mean, Helen,' he said, gently. 'You were having an affair with him.'

Ezra had anticipated a flood of tears but she straightened up and faced him defiantly, a smile on her lips.

'I am in love with Matthew.'

'And he is in love with you?'

'Yes. When the divorce comes through we will be married.'

Ezra wondered if this was her own idea or one shared by Matthew Sykes.

'And what about Luke?'

'I don't care what Luke thinks.'

'But you have cared about Luke, haven't you?'

Helen stood up.

'I think there's a bottle of port in the fridge. I wouldn't mind a glass. How about you?'

'Yes, why not.'

He watched her walk stiffly to the small fridge by the bed and take out the bottle.

'It's a bit cold,' she said, reaching on

the shelf for two glasses.

'That's all right . . . We were talking about Luke.'

'*You* were talking about Luke.'

'Helen. A man was murdered, a man who worked for your uncle. He went for Luke with a knife because Luke got his daughter pregnant. And Luke made a pass at you too, didn't he?'

'How much would you like? Is that enough?'

She appeared oblivious of his words.

'That's fine,' said Ezra, accepting the glass.

He watched her as she took a sip of her own.

'I quite enjoy an aged tawny, really. I wish we made more of it here.'

'Luke also had an affair with Katarina Soares,' Ezra continued, relentlessly. 'He broke it off when she told him she had been diagnosed with cancer.'

Helen gave a little sob.

'How do you know that?'

'Because Katarina Soares told me.'

'She told you herself?'

'Yes.'

'I don't believe it. They hate us. They'd say anything to turn us against each other.'

Ezra watched her hands. She was rubbing them together as if she were washing them.

'Tell me what happened that night when Amanda was here,' said Ezra.

Helen closed her eyes and began to rock slowly back and forth. She had picked up her glass again and was warming it between her palms.

'Auntie Amanda came to the quinta to speak with Matthew. She had found out about us. Luke must have told her.'

'When did Luke find out that you and Matthew were lovers?'

'I'm not sure. But looking back on it I can see now he was furious with his father. I mean really angry. He was determined to seduce me just out of spite. He didn't love me. He just wanted to get back at Matthew.'

'Why did you let him?'

'I don't know. I was flattered I suppose. A woman like me doesn't attract much attention. I had just come out of a brutalizing marriage. I was vulnerable. Matthew was away on one of his trips. Luke was here. After dinner one night he asked me when I was born. I thought he was going to talk about signs, you know the Zodiac, astrology. I told him and he got up from the table. When he came back he had a bottle of vintage port from my birth year. That's very romantic, you know. We joked about it, that he wasn't even a gleam in his father's eye when the wine was bottled. He showed me how they opened it with port tongs. You know, heating them up in the fire and applying them to the neck and then using a wet feather. The whole neck snaps off quite cleanly with the cork still intact. He decanted the bottle over a candle flame. The light made the wine look like blood. I remember watching his wrists. They seemed so strong. So in control. I must have consumed most of the bottle. Luke kept pouring and pouring while we were talking . . . classic situation, wouldn't you say? I don't really know what happened. The next thing I knew we were in bed together.'

'Go on.'

'He was so gentle that night. But the next day I felt awful. I'd betrayed the man I loved with his own son. I couldn't bring myself to tell Matthew and every time Luke came near me I wanted to throw up. And then he said he would tell his father if I didn't sleep with him again. He was only doing it to get revenge on Matthew, you see, because he thought that I was the cause of the marriage breaking up. But the seeds were there many years ago. They always are.'

'The other night, when Amanda slept here, why did she have the lawyer with her?'

'There were some financial dealings. I don't understand them. Amanda has her own money. She's quite wealthy in her own right. Her father was big in nitrate and iron ore. Chile, I believe. She was his only daughter. All Matthew's money is tied up in the quinta. He mortgaged the farm and the port in his warehouse in Vila Nova de Gaia. Mortgaged it all to pay for the new vineyards. Matthew asked her to lend him some money but she refused him. She had already lent him a large sum to finance the recontouring of the vineyard. He's already stretched to the limit with these bicentennial celebrations he's planned.'

Helen took a sip of port.

'I still don't understand why she came here,' said Ezra.

'She had found out about me, you see. She wanted to protect her interest in the quinta so she brought him papers to sign. She called in her loan. And she would only agree to a divorce if he signed the quinta over to her.'

'But I thought she hated the place.'

'It was just her way of getting back at Matthew. She has absolutely no interest in the port business.'

'But Matthew must have left the quinta while she was still here because he met me in Oporto. We had lunch together.'

'There was no way they could have remained under the same roof after what had passed between them. They would have killed each other. So Matthew did the gentlemanly thing. Instead of asking her to get out he left. If it had been me . . .'

She left the statement uncompleted, taking refuge in her glass once more.

'When did he leave?'

'The day after Auntie Amanda arrived.'

'She was here for three days. What did she do here?'

'Not much. She was on the phone a lot. She and the lawyer walked around the property. I imagine she was counting the barrels.'

'Did she ever speak to Alvaro Soares?'

'Not to my knowledge. Why do you ask?'

'I would imagine that if she thought she would gain control of the quinta she would also inherit the lawsuit,' said Ezra.

'Auntie Amanda didn't approve of the Soares. Especially her.'

'Did Matthew ever sign a document handing over the quinta to Amanda?'

'No. That was the last thing he would do. He loves this place. He went to Oporto to speak to his bankers to see if he could raise the extra money he needed.'

'If Amanda had gotten him to sign, and she took possession of the property, was it her intention to give it to Luke?'

'That's what Luke must have believed. But she had other ideas. Auntie Amanda is a control freak. She wants to have everyone under her thumb. Luke and she had a big argument in the lagar. I could hear them shouting from the house. I'm sure it was about the quinta.'

'How could you tell they were arguing?'

'I must confess, I did listen in. Luke thought it would amuse his mother to know that he had seduced me. That way he was her ally. But Amanda was furious when he told her. She left that night, dragging her lawyer in tow.'

'You told me before that she'd left in the morning.'

'What am I going to say to a guest? That she left in the middle of the night after a fight with her son?'

'Did you call Matthew at his club in Oporto and tell him what had happened?'

'Yes.'

'Everything?'

302

'Do you mean about my sleeping with Luke?'

'Yes.'

'I had to tell him before Auntie Amanda could.'

'And how did he react?'

'He was very upset, naturally. He said he would come back first thing in the morning and we'd talk about it.'

'How did that conversation go?'

Helen shrugged and sighed.

'We have some things to work out.'

'So you haven't burnt your bridges.'

'I told you. We have some things to work out.'

Ezra felt like an interrogating detective. He'd had enough experience in his career as an amateur sleuth, being on the receiving end of such cross-examinations, that he knew when to press for an answer and when to move on to another subject.

'And after you called Matthew?'

'When Auntie Amanda had gone I began closing up the house as I usually do. Luke has his own keys so he could let himself in. He's always out late. I was locking up the front gate when I heard voices coming from the shed where the lagar is. The door was open and there were no lights on. I could hear a girl's voice and then a man's. She was pleading with him, asking him to stop. It was Luke with one of the serving girls.'

'Anna Figueira, Gertrudes' daughter.'

'How did you know?'

'Just a guess. I noticed she had bruises on her upper arms.'

'Yes, it was Anna. Luke was forcing himself on her. He had her pinned to the wall and his hand was . . . So I called to him to stop. Anna broke free and ran out of the shed in tears.'

'What time was this?'

'About ten fifteen, maybe ten thirty. I don't know. It was late.'

'So you and Luke are together in the dark out there in the lagar. What happened then?'

'He treated it as if it were all a big joke. He told me about the fight he had had with his mother. He said she had taken off her wedding ring and told him to give it back to his father. Luke said to her, 'Why don't you do it yourself?' And she said, 'Because I never want to see any of you again.' Then he held up the ring to me and said, 'I bet *you'd* like to have this. Why don't you try it on? See if it fits. It's what you want, isn't it?' He pushed it into my hand and he kept on repeating it. 'Try it on. See if it fits. You'll be married to him. What do I call you then? Mother? Shall I call you Mother?' I just lost my temper. I threw the ring back at him. It hit him on the shoulder and must have landed in the lagar.'

Ezra recalled the photos that had hung in Maddox' mobile darkroom. Night shots of Luke and Helen embracing and walking together in a vineyard. They must have come from the same roll of film that Maddox had surreptitiously shot of him and Matthew in Oporto. It could have been the night before he arrived or his first night at the quinta, when he had happened upon Helen praying in the chapel.

But, Ezra realized, it could only have been his first night in the Douro because Maddox had arrived in Pinhão the same time he did. Katarina Soares was waiting to show the photographer the way up to Quinta do Coteiro.

'Luke didn't have dinner with me the night I arrived,' he said. 'Do you know where he went that night?'

'I have no idea.'

'I think you have.'

'Luke often goes out on his own at night, chasing every little totty in the town,' said Helen, bitterly.

'I think he was with you that night, Helen. The night after Amanda left.'

'I don't want to continue this conversation any longer, Mr Brant.'

She rose from her chair and straightened her skirt.

'I'll have Vasco bring your things down.'

'One last thing, please. I'm asking you this for Matthew's sake. The day I arrived, was Albino Sousa in the house at any time?'

She thought for a moment.

'Yes. Matthew had asked him to pick up a pair of shoes from the mender's. A cousin of Albino's is a cobbler in Pinhão.'

'Did he leave the shoes with you?'

'No. I asked him to put them directly into Matthew's wardrobe.'

'Did you actually see the shoes?'

'Well, no. They were in a box, but if you think he stole them we can always check and make sure they're there.'

'There's no need,' said Ezra.

Another piece of the puzzle had fallen into place.

★ ★ ★

Ezra lay on the bed in the guest cottage, shoes off, hands behind his head, thinking about Katarina. He had packed his belongings and Vasco had brought his suitcase down from the main house, carrying Ezra's suits separately on their hangers.

As they drove down to the guest house Ezra had asked the vineyard manager if he had been at Albino Sousa's funeral? Yes, he had. Had Matthew Sykes and Luke returned to the quinta? No, they had taken the Mercedes and driven in to see the marquee in the vineyard. They would be back for dinner.

Lying on the bed as the evening sky outside the window turned lilac, he wondered if he would ever see Katarina again. The Soares and the Sykes, the Capulets and the Montagues, only in this tragedy Juliet would die and Romeo would live to carry on his carefree, womanizing ways.

Ezra had learned much from his conversation with Helen. Matthew Sykes was in debt to the bank and his wife was not prepared to bail him out unless he signed over the quinta to her. He had refused to do this. Amanda would only offer him a divorce on that condition. How convenient if Amanda had died of a snake bite. The viper had been put in the bed in which she had slept. She had left suddenly in the middle of the night before she had intended. Had a murderer's plan been thwarted by that premature departure?

Yet he could not believe that Matthew Sykes would resort to such a strategy to rid himself of a wife he no longer loved, even one who schemed to take his beloved quinta away from him. The only possible way the snake could have found its way into a newly made bed would be if someone had put it there.

And that someone must have been Albino Sousa.

He must have carried it into the house in the shoe box containing Sykes' newly mended shoes. But what reason would Sykes' farm manager have for putting a poisonous snake in Amanda's bed other than on instructions from Matthew Sykes himself? Unless someone else had paid him to do it.

But Albino Sousa was dead. Murdered not that many hours after he would have secreted the snake in between the sheets.

Who had the most to gain from Amanda's death? Helen would be rid of the one person who stood in the way of what she perceived to be her future happiness. At one stroke she would eliminate a threat to Matthew's proprietorship of the quinta and the one person who prevented her from marrying the man she loved.

Yet from Ezra's reading of her she had neither the guile nor the will to see such an action through.

And then there was Luke. Was he ruthless enough to order the murder of his own mother? He had proved himself to be heartless and without conscience in his dealings with other women . . .

Or had Albino Sousa acted on his own initiative — to revenge himself on the Sykes family for the dishonouring of his daughter and the terrible accident that had befallen his brother on their land?

Ezra felt tired. He realized that he had not eaten since breakfast, apart from the sliced pineapple he had shared with Katarina in bed. He lay back on the pillow and closed his eyes. Tomorrow the festivities would begin. The guests would be arriving and the family would be caught up in their roles as hosts. He had not accomplished the task that Matthew Sykes had set him. Somehow the dynamics of the situation had changed with the death of Albino Sousa. That crime did not fit the pattern of the minor acts of mischief and vandalism that had plagued the quinta in the weeks leading up to the bicentennial celebrations. Even the snake in his bed (was it really meant for Amanda or was he the intended victim?) could be interpreted as a message rather than a murder attempt.

What could he tell Matthew Sykes? Small wonder the man was not that interested in what Ezra had to report on his return to the quinta. He had been in a foul mood, preoccupied with revelations of the family triangle and the financial problems that threatened to destroy his life's work.

Even Ezra's research into the Baron de Forrester had not progressed as well as it might have done. He found himself being sidetracked, unwittingly drawn into the Sykes' family saga; and he himself had complicated matters further by involving himself romantically with Katarina Soares. In this he had given no thought to his own personal safety. If Alvaro Soares were to discover that he had slept with his wife what fate might befall him? They just might find another corpse in the Douro.

In his soporific state Ezra's mind disengaged and his thoughts flowed freely

311

. . . Images bubbled to the surface of his consciousness like newspaper headlines: Ezra Brant shot by jealous husband . . . Body found floating face-down in the Douro like Albino Sousa. Or maybe never found, like Joseph James Forrester. There would be no dipping of flags by the ships in the harbours of Oporto and Lisbon for him. No plaques or public monuments, just a stack of scrapbooks, one for each year of his columns in the *Toronto Examiner*, as a legacy that his son would probably consign to the attic alongside his own grade school paintings and report cards. A short obituary in the local newspaper, a mention of his book, *Footprints In My Wine*, and an account of his mysterious death, presumed to be at the hands of a disgruntled producer whose wines he had savaged in print . . . And then there was the cave with its magical paintings that must have dated back to the First Bronze age. He wondered if Joseph Forrester knew of their existence from his solitary journeys along the river. There was no reference to them in the letters and had they been discovered they would have been exploited as a tourist attraction by now.

Tourist attraction! Yes, of course. Alvaro Soares and his wife knew of the cave and they knew that it ran under the vineyard that Matthew Sykes was replanting — a vineyard Sousa believed to be rightfully his and was taking court action to get back. The cave and its Palaeolithic paintings were of far greater value to him than the port that could be produced above . . .

Ezra was jolted back to reality by the sound of a car driving up the hill towards the quinta. He looked at his watch. He had been dozing for twenty minutes. The sky had turned plum-coloured and the first stars of the night were visible as tiny points of light.

He could see Sykes' black Mercedes bumping up the hill, the beams from its headlights chopping like twin swords through the gathering darkness. He felt a curious sense of excitement, knowing that he needed one more piece of information to confirm his theory about why Albino Sousa had been murdered and who was his killer. But the real question was: once he had the answer what was he going to do about it? Would he honour his agreement with Matthew Sykes and tell him or would he go straight to the tiny Inspector Cruz and let the police deal with it? Or would he say nothing until the celebrations were over and let matters take their course? It was not his responsibility and any revelations at this point could compromise the festivities Matthew Sykes had planned for his guests.

He wondered what had transpired between the detective and Sykes. Did they reach an agreement that the investigation would be put on a back burner until the anniversary celebrations were over? Albino Sousa was in his grave. He had nowhere to go and there was nothing to be gained by cancelling such an event at the eleventh hour after the months of planning. All the leading players were there. If one of them were to disappear now it would only point up their guilt. Inspector Cruz could afford to wait for three days.

But could he in all conscience just set aside the information he had discovered and return to Toronto knowing that a murder had been committed? Perhaps he should tell Inspector Cruz what he had learned and let the tiny detective deal with the consequence. That was his job. But out of sympathy for his host the least he could do would be to tell Matthew Sykes what he had deduced and let him come to terms with those revelations as he saw fit.

And better to do it now before the party began because, knowing what he did now, he could not be a silent witness to the proceedings to come.

Ezra dressed carefully, rehearsing in his mind how he would break the news to Sykes. Should he ask to speak to him in private or do it over dinner in front of Luke and Helen? He needed one more element to be sure of his facts.

He packed his suitcase, knowing that he might have to leave that night, and made his way up the vineyard path to the house. He would choose his moment and if Luke and Helen were there then so be it. He checked his watch. It was already 8.15 p.m.

★ ★ ★

As he entered the house Ezra was surprised by the sound of unfamiliar voices coming from the living room. He could hear Matthew Sykes in animated conversation with a man and a woman. The man had an American accent; he sounded as if he came from one of the southern states.

'Ah, Ezra, do come in and let me introduce you to Schuyler Dufresne,' Sykes called to him as he entered the living room. 'Comes from your side of the pond. This is Ezra Brant, a distinguished wine writer from Canada. He thinks well of our port which also makes him highly discerning.'

The tanned and athletic man who stood in front of Ezra was dressed in an ice-cream-coloured suit and pale blue shirt. He extended his hand revealing a gold identity bracelet.

'Schuyler Dufresne, from Atlanta,

Georgia. I'm a dental surgeon and this is my wife, Louise Dufresne. We pronounce it the French way, not Dufrez-nee like the former quarterback of Michigan State.'

'Ezra Brant, from Toronto.'

'Oh Toronto! Weren't you at a convention a couple of years ago in Toronto, Schuyler?'

Her voice was piping and as enthusiastic as a cheerleader's.

'That was Toledo, honey.'

Ezra shook their hands. Louise Dufresne, a small, anorexic woman with bleached-blond hair, clad entirely in silk and expensive designer accessories, fanned herself with a handkerchief with her left hand while dangling the fingers of her right in a glass of ice water.

'Mr Dufresne buys vintage port for a syndicate of dentists and doctors in Georgia,' explained Sykes. 'I'm happy to say that they are enthusiastic fans of Quinta do San Pedro.'

'Two hundred and fifty cases last year, Mr Brant. I personally have every vintage this quinta has produced since 1900, bar three. That's why I'm here. To fill in the gaps. I'm trying to extract from Mr Sykes, if you'll pardon a dental joke, a case from my wife's birth year. It's okay, honey, I'm not going to tell them the vintage but it's a great one, Mr Brant.'

'I'm sure that can be arranged,' said Sykes. 'My son Luke will be down in a moment, so why don't we all go into dinner?'

Ezra quickly realized Sykes was treating the American dentist with the studied courtesy extended to a valued customer. His name had not been on the original list of guests so he must have turned up unexpectedly at the last moment. Sykes must have given him and his wife the room Ezra had occupied.

The table had been set for six and Helen was already in the dining room when they entered. After further introductions they sat down and immediately Schuyler Dufresne began to tell Ezra about the magnitude of his wine cellar.

'I keep the port in a special room, a little colder than the main cellar for my reds and whites, you understand. I'm a Burgundy man myself but a lot of my friends prefer claret.'

He pronounced the word without its final 't' and Ezra glanced over at Sykes who was intent on avoiding his eyes.

'Every St Martin's Day I hold a big Bordeaux tasting at our summer house in Savannah. Collectors fly in from every corner of the United States, Mr Brant. Last year it was all the 1945s, twenty-one in all, magnums of each of the First Growth and the better Seconds. You might have read about it in *The Wine Spectator*. One heck of a vintage, 1945. I guess the good Lord wanted to show us there was redemption after a war like that. I invited Michael Broadbent and he was going to come but he had an auction to conduct in London. He sent me a very fine letter saying how much he regretted not being able to attend. Anyway, I was sitting there, looking down the table, with a '45 in one hand and a '45 in the other hand. I tell you, I felt just like Billy the Kid.'

He slapped the table and roared with laughter while Louise Dufresne smiled the smile of a wife who had heard the anecdote more times than she cared to remember.

Ezra did not have the heart to tell Schuyler Dufresne that Billy the Kid's weapon of choice was a double action Colt .38 revolver — a piece of the trivia his gadfly mind absorbed like a sponge. He got the distinct impression that Louise Dufresne was kicking her husband under the table.

'Tell them about your other hobby, dear,' she said, smiling through gritted teeth.

'Oh that. They don't want to hear about that, honey.'

'On the contrary,' said Sykes, setting the decanter of tawny port in motion around the table.

'Well, I guess I have this kind of collector's instinct. I collect the names of murder victims.'

The room fell silent. Matthew Sykes held the decanter in mid-air and stared in horrified fascination at his American guest. Ezra looked at Schuyler Dufresne with new interest.

'How do you mean?' he asked.

'I have this theory, you see, Mr Brant. I believe that certain people have a predisposition to become victims because of the name they were given at birth. The Christian name, the name they were baptized with, you understand. So I read the newspapers. I get papers from all across America and whenever I see a story about murder I clip it out and make a note of the victim's name in my computer. Where and how they were killed, the city or town, and then I analyse them to see if there is a pattern. I've got over 12,000 names in my computer, Mr Brant.'

'And what are your conclusions?'

'It's too soon to tell but I can say one thing that I think you'll find very interesting. Names you find in the Good Book, they don't show up as the victims of violent crime very often. No, sir. So, statistically, you two gentlemen don't have much to worry about. Matthew and Ezra, you'll be just fine. That's why Louise and I have given all our children names from the Bible.'

'Seven,' interjected the proud mother, 'and all boys.'

Ezra was on the point of asking how many 'Schuylers' the dentist had come across in his research but he resisted the temptation and slid his glass towards Matthew Sykes who still had the decanter poised a foot above the table.

'Perhaps I should ask Anna to serve now,' said Helen, rising from her chair. 'I'm sure Luke won't mind if we start without him.'

Anna arrived with a tray of plates and a tureen of piping hot watercress soup.

Ezra drank more than he usually did that night. Dufresne continued to monopolize the conversation and had no interest in anything that either he, Matthew or Luke, who eventually turned up just as the main course was served, had to say. Helen said nothing throughout the meal. She just gazed at Matthew Sykes and hardly touched her food.

It soon became obvious to Ezra there would be no opportunity to speak to his host that night so he contrived to slide gracefully out and spend the rest of the evening in the blissful solitude of the guest house.

'What time is it?' Ezra asked when Schuyler Dufresne was preoccupied with the newly extracted cork from a bottle of 1977 Santo Pedro port. 'I'm afraid my watch has stopped.'

He addressed the question to Matthew Sykes and he observed him carefully as he reached into the fob pocket of his waistcoat and withdrew his pocket watch.

'Good heavens, it's almost midnight. Where has the time gone?'

'What a beautiful watch!' exclaimed Louise Dufresne. 'May I see it?'

'It was my grandfather's,' said Sykes, handing it to her.

A short length of chain dangled from the ring that protected the winder.

'If you don't mind, Matthew, I think I'm going to retire,' said Ezra.

'Yes, it's going to be a big day tomorrow. The bus will arrive with the visitors from Pinhão first thing for the naming ceremony. I'll see you in the morning.'

Ezra said his goodnights and left them

at the table. He winked at Helen on the way out and the last thing he heard was Schuyler requesting a pair of port tongs. He wanted to show his host that he had mastered the art of removing the cork cleanly from an old bottle of port by the application of red-hot metal tongs placed under the flange of the neck.

Workmen were hanging bunting by lantern-light along the walls of the quinta as Ezra left the house. He breathed deeply in the crisp night air.

The last piece of the puzzle had fallen into place.

★   ★   ★

In the darkness of the guest cottage Ezra, somewhat the worse for the amount of tawny port he had consumed, lay under the blankets in darkness, staring at the ceiling. He found himself agitated and on edge. He wondered how much Inspector Cruz had learned about Albino Sousa's murder. There was so much unfinished business here. He knew he would be leaving tomorrow before the celebrations had got into full swing. He would never see Katarina Soares again and this saddened him. He experienced a sense of deep loneliness and for the first time he understood how Joseph Forrester must have felt, cut off from his family, ostracized by his English peers because of his firmly held convictions about port, alone in a foreign land. Is it any wonder the man spent so much time exploring the Douro with only a mule for company?

He slipped into a troubled sleep and the dream he had of Forrester drowning in the Douro's raging waters returned. At first it was Forrester battling the torrent as the boatman's oar pushed him under the water and then it was his face he saw. He was drowning and Helen and Katarina and a woman who could have been Amanda Sykes floated by calling to him like sirens. He kept reaching for the oar as the current sucked him under and then he could feel its weight against his chest. He saw the leering face of Albino Sousa standing on the rocks above him and then the figure changed to Luke Sykes. And then it became Alvaro Soares.

Ezra awoke bathed in perspiration. His throat felt parched. He had broken one of his cardinal rules last night. He had not consumed a glass of water before he retired.

He eased his legs out of bed and stood on the cold wood floor. The sun glowed around the edges of the curtains. He opened the door to the fridge and took out a bottle of sparkling water. He poured himself a glass and drank the contents in a few gulps. It tasted salty and for one moment he wondered if it had been poisoned. Then he laughed grimly to himself, remembering what Schuyler Dufresne had told him: his biblical name would protect him from acts of violence.

When he had showered and shaved he dressed and packed his toiletries. Since he had to return the Forrester letters he decided to read them through again and type into his laptop those passages he thought he might need for his book.

Rereading the correspondence Ezra was struck by the man's fierce dedication to his life's work. Forrester approached port as if it were more than a mere alcoholic beverage. It was a way of life for a people, not the English shippers sitting around the mahogany dining table at the Factory House, but the farmers of the Douro who had to work the tortuous slopes that baked like ovens in summer and froze cold enough to crack granite in winter. The men who dug in the soil, oblivious of flies the size of humming birds, a wind that could blind and the dead weight of the grape hods on their shoulders. Men terrified of the evil spirits that lurked behind the rocks and in mountain springs, those lost souls of the dead searching for a living body through which they could be reincarnated. Men fearful of the Devil who could carry off a child or the family pig and shivered with fright in bed at the sound of galloping horses in the night. The Baron de Forrester might have painted the portraits of the rich and titled but his heart was in the high mountains with these illiterate farmers.

It was almost ten o'clock when Ezra put the Forrester letters back into their waterproof pouch and tied the strings. He slid the pouch into his jacket pocket and his fingers touched Katarina's lighter. He took it out, flipped the top and pressed the button. A blue flame with a yellow heart leapt out of the nozzle. He passed his fingers over the flame, feeling its warmth. How would he get it back to Katarina? Perhaps he should keep it, the only palpable object he had to remind him of her and the day they had spent together.

The sound of a heavy motor labouring up the hill past the guest house made him realize that it was time to join the festivities. Matthew Sykes' guests had arrived from Oporto and the vine-naming ceremony would soon begin.

On his way up to the house, Ezra noticed that the bus was leading a convoy of cars. It looked like a funeral procession rather than a celebration. They were heading in the direction of the new vineyard and, from the point where he stood, Ezra could see the marquee. The canvas wall facing the river had been rolled up revealing rows of gilded opera chairs on green outdoor carpeting.

Workmen in blue overalls were setting up tables behind the chairs in the marquee. The wind was playing havoc with the tablecloths that billowed like spinnakers before they were weighted down.

Ezra could see Luke directing operations and Matthew, standing next to a podium, testing the microphone.

'One, two, three, four, Mary had a little lamb . . . '

The amplified words echoed off the hillside, strangely disembodied.

The bus was lurching its way along the track leading into the vineyard, followed by a line of cars. Ezra began to walk towards the marquee. The bus had stopped and its passengers were alighting. Men in suits and women in hats and white gloves. Car doors opened and a mass of people began to move towards the vineyard. The route had been marked with bunting. A red carpet had been laid between the rows of young vines so that shoes would not be sullied by the rocky, sandy soil.

Ezra had half a mind to leave there and then. He did not relish the prospect of having to sit through the speeches, the ceremonies and all the self-congratulation knowing that he would be calling the man of the hour a murderer.

He made his way along the carpet to the marquee. The guests had already begun to seat themselves on the chairs. The front row had been reserved for dignitaries whom Luke was escorting to their seats. His father was standing at the podium, smiling broadly and waving to colleagues and friends. He caught Ezra's eye and made a thumbs-up sign in his direction.

Ezra smiled wanly in return and took his place at the end of the back row. A man with a video camera was recording the event, panning along the row of seats. Preoccupied, Ezra did not hear Schuyler Dufresne approach him.

'I said, good morning, Mr Brant. Mind if we squeeze in next to you there?'

'Not at all,' said Ezra.

He stood up to allow the Dufresnes to pass.

'Missed you at breakfast,' said the dentist.

'Yes,' said Ezra. 'I thought I'd sleep in.'

'Ladies and gentlemen, if you'll kindly take your seats . . . '

Matthew Sykes was preparing to get the proceedings underway.

The animated crowd fell silent as Matthew Sykes began to speak.

'Ladies and gentleman. I would like to thank you for making this journey to Quinta do Santo Pedro today to help us celebrate our two hundredth birthday. Our journey has been somewhat longer. Two years after the French Revolution my great-great-grandfather purchased this estate and members of my family have worked the land in an unbroken line since then. My son Luke, who will take over the reins of the company from me in the fullness of time, will be the sixth generation of Sykes to make port here in the Douro. We are part of this land and as you see in front of you we have made a commitment to it for the next two hundred years. Look around you and you will see a new vineyard here and to the east of our quinta. Your name will grace one of the vines in this vineyard as a memorial to this milestone for my family and the fruit it will bear . . . '

In the distance Ezra could hear a whirling sound that was becoming louder and louder. The seated guests began to murmur among themselves. Matthew Sykes, discomfited, stopped speaking and looked up in the sky for the source of the noise, shielding his eyes from the sun.

A helicopter rose from the hills to the west and climbed until it was positioned directly over the marquee. The noise of its rotor blades was intolerable and the guests rose from their seats with their hands pressed to their ears. It hovered over them like a malevolent bird of prey waiting to swoop on its quarry. The gale created by its blades kicked up clouds of choking dust and caused confusion for the guests on the ground. The wind flattened the roof of the marquee until the guy-lines could no longer take the strain. The canvas ripped and began to collapse upon itself. Guy-lines snapped and the poles fell inwards.

Guests fought their way out of the heaving canvas, blinded by dust and panicked by the noise. Women were crying and the men stood around impotently shaking their fists at the helicopter as it banked suddenly and veered away north.

Ezra helped Louise Dufresne to her feet and searched for Matthew Sykes. He had not moved from the podium. His face and clothes were covered with dust, his hair tousled. He stared at the wreckage of the marquee, unable to comprehend what had happened.

Luke grabbed the microphone.

'Ladies and gentlemen. Please, just stay calm. Our workmen will put everything right. We'll have everything back to normal in no time.'

★ ★ ★

Ezra dusted himself down and walked away from the vineyard. So Alvaro Soares had taken his revenge. He had spoiled Sykes' party. No doubt he would claim he was only overflying his own land and that the Englishman was trespassing by erecting a marquee on it. And maybe with a few bribes in the right places he might get away with it unless Matthew Sykes had more political clout in Lisbon than he did.

Ezra headed for the house, sick at heart. He did not want to have to confront Matthew Sykes now after such a fiasco. But he could not leave without letting the man know that his crime had come to light.

Helen was at the door when he arrived. Gertrudes and the kitchen staff, in their newly appointed black dresses and white lace collars, were craning out of the windows trying to find out what had happened. The expression on Helen's face told Ezra that she knew some new disaster had befallen the Sykes family.

'It was Soares, wasn't it?' she said.

'I imagine it was. Luke is trying to keep things going down there but I'm afraid I have to leave.'

'I'm sorry. Matthew will be disappointed.'

'It's because of Matthew. I have to talk to him, Helen.'

'Something's wrong, isn't it?'

'Yes.'

'Is he in any danger?'

Ezra sighed. Instead of replying directly, he said:

'Matthew came back here to the quinta that night, didn't he? Not the next morning as you said. He drove back in the middle of the night.'

'I don't know what you're talking about.'

'I think you do. Matthew came back and he slept in the guest cottage. I didn't see him until the next morning but I know he was on the property.'

'Let's go inside,' said Helen, glancing nervously at Gertrudes.

She led him into the living room and they sat down opposite each other across the coffee table. Ezra took out the pouch of letters and set them on the table.

'The Forrester letters,' he said. 'There's a passage in one of them where Forrester writes about the people of the Douro. How they never forget an insult or an injury. Also how superstitious they are.'

'What's that got to do with Matthew?'

Helen's face had hardened. The lines

around her mouth became more pronounced as she set her jaw in defiance.

'Let me explain then. Albino Sousa
didn't drown in the river. He was dead
before his body hit the water. He was
murdered, Helen.'

'How do you know that? You're not a
policeman, you're not a doctor. You didn't
see the body.'

'Those incidents that kept happening
around the quinta, the dead doves, the
dog, the fire, the snake in my bed, they
were Sousa's doing. But why would he do
these things? These are not the actions of
a man who wants to avenge himself on an
employer he holds responsible for turning
his brother into a walking vegetable. To
say nothing of the seduction of his
daughter by Luke. This was an orches-
trated campaign of threats for very
specific ends. Albino Sousa had made
some kind of a deal with Alvaro Soares
and I suspect I know why.'

'Go on.'

Helen sat with her hands clenched in
her lap, staring fixedly at him. He could
see her whole body trembling.

336

'Soares wants to get back the vineyards that Matthew has planted. He believes they belong to him and as you know the court battle has been going on for some years. But something happened that brought matters to a head and made it a matter of urgency that the ownership question be settled in his favour. When Luis Sousa, Albino's brother, had the tractor accident in the lower vineyard in June he inadvertently uncovered a cave which runs from the river, under the road and under the vineyard. When Albino found his brother pinned under the tractor he also found the shaft the bulldozer exposed that leads into the cave. He must have covered it up with the idea of coming back later once he got his brother to hospital. Only Luis' injuries were critical and he needed immediate medical assistance that could only be given in a major hospital. Matthew asked Soares if he could have Luis airlifted by helicopter to Oporto. Albino must have felt he owed Soares a great debt of gratitude for saving his brother's life. He probably told him about the cave.'

'What's so special about a cave?'

Ezra thought about his promise to Katarina. He had already divulged too much.

'Let's just say it's very important to Alvaro Soares.'

'So you're saying the Soares put Albino Sousa up to sabotaging Matthew's event.'

'Yes, but I imagine he would have had to sweeten the pot. Gratitude only goes so far. Look at it from Albino Sousa's point of view. His brother is almost killed in an accident in Matthew's vineyard. His daughter is deflowered by Luke. He begins to think that his family is cursed working at Quinta do Santo Pedro. Being a superstitious man he wants to leave but he doesn't know what to do. He unburdens himself to Alvaro Soares who sees a way to get at Matthew. Soares offers Albino money to stay on to wreak havoc around the quinta and maybe he promises him a job when the court case is won.'

'What has all this to do with Matthew being in danger?'

'I'm coming to that. Matthew didn't

come back immediately to the quinta when you phoned him that night to tell him about your conversation with Luke and the fight he had with his mother. Yet he rushed back the next night because he found out something. Somehow he learned that Albino Sousa was behind all the incidents. And he came back to kill him.'

The blood began to drain from Helen's face and he thought she was going to faint.

'What proof have you got?' she demanded.

'I was shown the cave yesterday. I came across a link from a gold chain on the floor. I have it in my pocket. I'm convinced it was part of Matthew's watch chain. You may have noticed last night at dinner his watch chain is broken.'

'What are you saying?'

'Let me take it back a bit. The night Sousa was killed I was at a cockfight. Katarina Soares drove me there. She picked me up on the road and asked me if I'd like to go with her. Albino Sousa was there too and so was Vasco. Both of them had birds who were fighting. Someone had tipped off the police about the fight because they raided the place. But they gave everyone enough time to clear out before they arrived. You could hear their siren for miles. Albino Sousa left on his bicycle with his rooster in a sack. The next morning his body is found in the Douro with a wound to the temple. And the sack he used for his bird is in Vasco's truck.'

'Then maybe it was Vasco who killed him — if he was murdered.'

'No. I think Vasco happened along *after* Albino had been killed. He must have found the sack at the side of the road and picked it up. The bicycle hasn't been found yet. It's probably at the bottom of the river.'

'What has all this got to do with Matthew?'

'I believe Matthew must have found out about the cave. He went looking for Albino Sousa and came across him cycling home. He stopped him and forced Albino to take him to the cave. There's an entrance down by the river where you can get in. Matthew had found out that Albino was in league with Soares and when they got to the cave he saw what Albino was trying to keep from him. That's when he lost it. He went for Albino and in the struggle he broke his watch chain and somehow Albino ended up with his head bashed in. Then Matthew threw his body into the river.'

'Remarkably perceptive, Ezra. But not exactly as it happened.'

Matthew Sykes stood in the doorway, pale and shaken. Dust had stuck to the sweat of his brow and dulled the colour of his green Harris tweed suit.

Helen sprang to her feet and rushed to his side to help him to a chair.

'Thank you, my dear.'

'Can I get you something? A glass of water? Brandy?'

'Water if you please.'

He smiled up at her and stroked her arm.

'I'm sorry it had to end like this,' said Ezra.

Sykes looked much older than his years now. A spent force, he sagged in his chair.

'In a way, I'm rather glad it was you,' he said.

He stared vacantly out of the window.

'I never intended it, you know.'

'No. I hardly think you would have invited me here if it had been premeditated,' said Ezra. 'Tell me what happened, Matthew.'

Sykes raised both hands and shook his head as if he didn't know where to begin.

'All I ever asked was loyalty. You treat them well, you listen to their problems, you take care of their families and they turn on you like vipers.'

'I remember you got a phone call just before I caught the train in Oporto to come here. You said you had to go to your lawyers' for a meeting.'

'Yes. Soares' people had sent them a new survey map that he had made redrawing the boundaries of our respective vineyard holdings. He said he was prepared to withdraw his claim to the property east of the quinta, where we pitched the marquee, if I would sign over to him the vineyard to the west. At first I thought this might be a way out of a

342

costly legal battle that was draining me. The vineyard to the west is smaller and the exposure to the sun is not as good as the other. I would have accepted that compromise until I saw the actual copy of the map. A small rectangular plot, about a half an acre in the corner nearest the road, had been pencilled off and the initials A. S. were written inside it. The lines and the initials had been rubbed out with an eraser but they were still clearly visible. Naturally, I assumed that 'A.S.' referred to Alvaro Soares. But when I thought more about it it didn't make sense since that son-of-a-bitch was after the whole vineyard, not just one small plot. And in the worst part of the vineyard at that. Then it came to me. Soares had promised Albino Sousa a portion of the vineyard for himself if he destroyed me.'

'But how did you find out about the cave?' asked Ezra.

'There was a lawyer's letter accompanying the map with rather curious wording. It stated that Sousa demanded the rights to everything above and below the ground on the property in question. Above and below the ground, mark you. This is not the usual language of vineyard leases. It led me to suspect that Soares thought there might be gold or some other precious stones on the property. But there is nothing of this nature in the area. It's only good for growing grapes. I reasoned that since he expressly used this wording there must be something under the ground that he wanted to get hold of. When Albino Sousa came to me carrying his brother in his arms he was almost incoherent but I recalled that he mentioned something about a cave. I took no notice of it at the time until I saw that lease.'

'And you know why Soares wanted that cave.'

'Yes,' said Sykes.

Helen came back into the room carrying a glass of water filled with ice cubes.

'Thank you, my dear.'

Sykes took a sip and placed the glass on the table in front of him. Helen sat protectively on the arm of his chair.

'How did you find Albino Sousa?' asked Ezra.

'I drove directly to his house in Cotas but he wasn't there. He padlocks his bicycle outside the front door for the neighbours to see. He's very proud of it. I should say 'was'. I was driving back here when I spotted him on the road. I don't know what came over me. I stopped the jeep and ordered him to put his bicycle in the back and come with me. I told him I would no longer pay wages to his brother Luis if he did not show me the cave. He pretended he didn't know what I was talking about at first but I said I would talk to his priest if he lied to me.'

Sykes reached for Helen's hand and held it.

'Tell him to leave, Matthew,' she pleaded.

He shook his head.

'No, they would find out sooner or later. It's better to get it off my chest now . . . We had a little trouble finding the entrance to the cave in the dark. I had a torch in the jeep but the rocks were slippery and there was a wind. When we got inside and I shone the beam on the walls it was the most beautiful sight I have ever seen. As I looked at those paintings I wept. And then the realization came to me of how Albino had betrayed me. I shone the torch in his eyes and I could see the hatred there. He pulled out his pruning knife and made a lunge for me. But he was blinded by the light and couldn't find me. I hit him as hard as I could with the torch and he went down like a sack of coal.'

Sykes gave Helen's hand a squeeze before he continued. She gave a little sob.

'Then I rolled the body into the water and threw the bicycle in after it.'

Something did not ring true in Ezra's mind. Detective Inspector Cruz had said a quantity of port had been found in Sousa's stomach. Yet there had been nothing to drink at the cockfight and he could not imagine the vineyard manager swigging from a bottle while he cycled home, nor Sykes and Sousa actually drinking together. And if Sykes had rolled the body into the river near the entrance to the cave it would have been found there or further downstream if it had floated on the current. Cruz had shown him on the map that the body was found below Alvaro Soares' vineyard.

'What are you going to do now?' Ezra asked.

'Turn myself in, I suppose.'

'No!' Helen gasped. 'You must tell him the truth.'

She was on her feet, the colour rising in her cheeks, her chest heaving.

'It's all right, Helen. I had every intention of killing him.'

'That's not true.'

'It doesn't matter.'

'It matters to me, Matthew.'

Tears were coursing down her cheeks.

'It's better this way,' said Sykes.

He took her hand and kissed it.

'If you're not going to tell him, I will,' she replied defiantly and pulled her hand away.

She moved to the window and with her back to the two men she began to talk.

'Matthew didn't kill Albino. He was alive when he brought him here to the guest house.'

'Helen, it won't help matters.'

She wheeled around angrily.

'I'm not going to let you do this, Matthew. Mr Brant, please listen to what I have to say. Matthew called me from the cave on his cellphone . . .'

Ezra remembered the phone ringing in the night.

' . . . He told me he had had a fight with Albino and that he had knocked him out. He was going to bring him back to the guest house and I was to meet him there with antiseptic and bandages. Albino was still unconscious when Matthew carried him in and laid him on the bed.'

'You're positive he was still alive?' interjected Ezra.

'A man doesn't groan if he's dead,' said Helen. 'Matthew told me what he had done and why he did it. How Albino was behind all the terrible things that happened here. How he had deceived us all this time, scheming with Mr Soares. A Judas in our midst and after all Matthew had done for him and his brother. Matthew was shaking and he didn't know what to do. I told him to go and wash and I would take care of Albino.'

'No, Helen, please. I beg you.'

Helen was not to be deterred by the feeble entreaty.

'When Matthew was in the bathroom and I could hear the water running, I took the pillow from under Albino's head and pressed it to his face until he stopped moving.'

Matthew groaned and slumped in his chair.

'Oh, my God, Helen.'

She stood erect and triumphant, a tall figure framed by the window.

'There is nothing I wouldn't do for you, Matthew.'

'How did you dispose of the body?'

'It had to look like an accident. I sat him up and poured a bottle of port down his throat. Then we carried him to the jeep and drove him down to the river at the bottom of Mr Soares' property. I wanted it to look like he had slipped on the rocks and fallen in.'

'If the police considered it murder rather than an accident you wanted the suspicion to fall on Alvaro Soares. Am I right?' said Ezra.

Helen and Sykes exchanged glances.

'It's only what he deserves,' said Helen. 'You fill his stomach with Soares' tawny port and dump the body near Quinta do Coteiro.'

'Matthew doesn't deserve this, Mr Brant.'

'A man has been murdered, Helen. The punishment is a little more than he deserved,' replied Ezra.

Before Helen could respond there was a gentle knock at the door. Anna Figueira stepped into the room, oblivious of the charged atmosphere.

'There is a visitor in the hall, Senhor Sykes.'

'Who is it, Anna?' asked Helen.

'Senhora Katarina Soares.'

Ezra experienced a tremor of excitement at the sound of her name.

Matthew Sykes rose from his chair, ran a hand through his hair and buttoned his jacket.

'Ask her to come in, Anna,' he said, gravely.

'Matthew . . .', protested Helen, but he put up a hand to silence her.

Anna held the door open and Katarina stepped into the room. She was wearing a cream-coloured suit but her head was bare. Helen gasped when she saw the bald skull feathered with a soft, blond fuzz. Sykes took in the sight and tried to look away.

Katarina smiled at Ezra and then she addressed herself to Sykes.

'Mr Sykes, I have come to apologize for my husband. What he did was not right. You and he have your differences but this is not the way to settle them.'

'I admire your courage, madam,' said Sykes, 'but your husband's actions were a deliberate provocation and it is he who should be here to apologize. Thank God no one was hurt, that's all I can say.'

'My husband is a proud man. I assure you that he will make amends.'

'We will settle this between our lawyers,' said Sykes. 'Now if you'll excuse me I must return to my guests.'

Katarina nodded.

'Land, money, revenge. It is of no value

in the end. There is nothing more important than life,' she said.

Ezra watched her walk out of the room. 'I'm leaving too, Matthew,' he said. 'I'm going to see Detective Inspector Cruz. Perhaps it would be easier on you if you called him first. If I am any judge of character I know you'll do the right thing.'

Matthew Sykes accepted his outstretched hand and shook it. He looked tired and worn. He smiled sadly.

'Thank you, Ezra. Don't think badly of us. Sometimes history gets in the way of one's better instincts. I envy you in the New World, unburdened by the past.'

'Good luck,' said Ezra.

Sykes nodded.

'Goodbye, Helen.'

She said nothing but stared coldly at him.

In the courtyard he heard the sound of Katarina's Mercedes starting up. He ran to the gates and called to her. The top was down and she had put on her turban hat.

'Katarina,' he said, 'may I ask a favour?'

'What is it?'

'I need a lift to Pinhão. I'm leaving.'

'Of course. Get in.'

'I just have to pick up my case from the guest cottage down there. Does your husband know you came here?' asked Ezra, as they drove onto the highway.

'Alvaro told me what had happened and he laughed. He never apologizes.'

'That was an inspiration, to take your hat off.'

Katarina smiled.

'You have to use every weapon at your disposal, my friend. Now they know I am dying they will be a little more forgiving. Are you really leaving?'

'Yes. There is no reason for me to stay now. Except you.'

'You are very sweet, Ezra, and I will think of you. But in the time I have left I want it to be full of light. No regrets, no thinking of what might have been.'

'I understand.'

They drove in silence under a cloudless blue sky that seemed to go on forever. The vineyards, the wind-smoothed granite slopes, the wiry ilex bushes — a landscape that dwarfed the harvesters who moved slowly across it under the sun. Apart from the tarmacadamed road it was no different now than it had been over 150 years ago when Joseph Forrester travelled the hills by mule with his theodolite and his chains.

'Do you have one wish before you go?' asked Katarina.

Before he could answer she said: 'Apart from making love. It would be too sad for me.'

'There is one thing,' said Ezra. 'Take me to your favourite place in the Douro.'

He wanted to see one last time where the Baron de Forrester had drowned, to pay his final respects.

They drove up to San Salvador do Mundo and stood on the top of the mountain looking down at the Valeira dam. The water was incredibly blue, almost purple like the skin of a ripe plum. Ezra breathed deeply.

The only matter that needed closure now was the mystery of the Baron's death. That he had been drowned in the Douro was incontestable. But it had not been an accident. It might have been the Duke of Saldanha's men, taking revenge because Forrester had thwarted plans for the enforced marriage of Dona Antonia Ferreira's daughter and the Duke's son. Or it could have been a conspiracy among certain English port shippers to rid themselves of a troublesome reformer who threatened their lucrative trade. It might have been a secret service agent of the British (or the French) ordered to eliminate a spy who had outlived his usefulness. Or perhaps it was an unknown assassin who learned that Forrester was travelling with a money belt of gold to ransom a kidnapped boy.

Staring down at the river that had claimed Joseph James Forrester's life he ran over the possibilities. Given the Baron's stature in the community and his friendship with the King himself there was little likelihood that the Duke of Saldanha would have struck at him so long after the abortive abduction. Nor would Forrester's peers in the port trade — his fellow English shippers — be driven to plot his assassination. If anything his zealous pursuit of purity had given the Douro and its wine an enormous amount of publicity and had kept his less scrupulous competitors on the straight and narrow. Blunt Yorkshireman that he was, Forrester would have had little sympathy for the backstairs intrigues of government. Given his love for his adopted country it was inconceivable that he would spy against the Portuguese for the British secret service, let alone the French.

No, Forrester's death must have been planned and executed by the boatman who ferried the party downriver. His motive was the gold that Forrester carried in his money belt. He had lashed the rudder the wrong way to negotiate the rapids so the boat would hit the gorge wall. The boatman had not acted alone. His accomplice would have waited downriver for the body to float by. Relieved of the gold the body was thrown back into the river to move on the current down past the port lodges of Vila Nova de Gaia and out into the Atlantic Ocean.

May he rest in peace.

'What are you thinking?' asked Katarina.

Ezra turned to face her.

'About an Englishman who gave his life for the Douro.'

'Are you talking about Matthew Sykes?'

Ezra was about to say that it was Joseph James Forrester whom he was thinking about but instead he just nodded.

'By the way, I still have your lighter. I should give it back to you.'

'I don't need it,' said Katarina. 'Throw it into the river.'

'It's an expensive lighter!'

'Then the pleasure will be all the greater.'

'Okay. Here goes.'

With a swinging, overarm motion he hurled the lighter high into the air. It flashed momentarily in the sun and then disappeared.

Ezra felt a curious sense of peace. It was almost as if he was returning Joseph Forrester's gold to him.

The river below the dam continued to flow into the Atlantic. Its surface was dappled with sunlight like so many gold coins.

'I can go now,' he said.

THE END

We do hope that you have enjoyed reading this large print book.

Did you know that all of our titles are available for purchase?

We publish a wide range of high quality large print books including:
Romances, Mysteries, Classics
General Fiction
Non Fiction and Westerns

Special interest titles available in large print are:
The Little Oxford Dictionary
Music Book, Song Book
Hymn Book, Service Book

Also available from us courtesy of Oxford University Press:
Young Readers' Dictionary
(large print edition)
Young Readers' Thesaurus
(large print edition)

For further information or a free brochure, please contact us at:
Ulverscroft Large Print Books Ltd.,
The Green, Bradgate Road, Anstey,
Leicester, LE7 7FU, England.
Tel: (00 44) **0116 236 4325**
Fax: (00 44) **0116 234 0205**

Other titles in the
Linford Mystery Library:

DEATH OF A LOW HANDICAP MAN

Brian Ball

When Tom Tyzack is viciously beaten to death with a golf club on the local golf course, PC Arthur Root, the local village bobby, is in the unenviable position of having to question his fellow club members. He is regarded with scorn by the detective in charge of the case, and the latter's ill-natured attitude toward the suspects does little to assist him in solving the mystery. But it is Root who, after a second brutal murder, stumbles on the clue that leads to the discovery of the murderer's identity.